JEWEL society

keep friends close, emeralds closer

by **Hope McLean**

Scholastic Inc.

For Maddie, who would fit right in with the Jewels!

ISBN 978-0-545-60764-3

12 11 10 9 8 7 6 5 4 3 2 1   13 14 15 16 17 18/0

Printed in the U.S.A.   40
This edition first printing, October 2013
Previously published as *Jewel Thieves: Keep Friends Close, Emeralds Closer*
Book design by Natalie C. Sousa

Chapter One

Willow Albern shot the basketball from the right side of the court. It formed a perfect arc, then dropped into the basket with a *swish*.

"Nice shot, Willow!" her friend Erin Fischer cheered.

Lili Higashida ran up to the girls, panting. "I hate when we play basketball in gym class!" she complained. "I'm too short!"

"You're about the same size as I am," Erin pointed out. "Besides, as long as we have Willow on our team, we don't need to do much. She's the best player in class."

Their friend Jasmine Johnson motioned to them. "Come on, guys," she urged, her curly brown hair bouncing. "Blue team's got the ball!"

The four girls ran down the court with the rest of their teammates, all dressed in their ruby-red Martha Washington School gym shirts. The other team wore blue vests over their red shirts.

A girl on the blue team had control of the ball. She dribbled down the court to make a layup shot but Willow intercepted her, took the ball, and headed back down the court to the other basket. Jasmine sprinted ahead of her, waving her arms.

"Willow! Over here! I'm open!"

But instead of passing the ball to Jasmine, Willow stopped near the foul line. She reached out over the girl covering her and shot another basket, her ponytail bouncing on her head as she jumped. Once again, the ball cleared the net with a satisfying *swoosh*.

A loud whistle sounded.

"That's game! Class time is over," cried Ms. McKnight, their gym teacher. "Red team wins!"

The girls on the red team cheered and high-fived each other — but Erin noticed that Jasmine didn't slap Willow's hand.

"What's the matter?" Erin asked as the team started breaking up.

"Nothing," Jasmine said sullenly. "It's just — sometimes Willow acts like there's nobody else on the team but her, you know?"

Willow overheard. "That's not true!" she protested.

"Then why didn't you pass me the ball?" Jasmine countered.

"Because I had a clear shot," Willow replied.

"You did not," Jasmine said. "Annmarie was covering you."

"All right, girls!" Ms. McKnight announced to the class. "I want you to walk a few laps around the gym to cool down."

The girls fell in step behind their classmates. Nobody said anything for a minute.

"Please don't fight, guys," Lili said finally. "I mean, we won the game, right?"

"No, *Willow* won the game," Jasmine said. "She made all the baskets. It's just like quiz bowl."

"Wait a second," Erin said. "That's not true. We *all* answer questions during a match."

The four friends were members of the school's elite quiz bowl team, called the Jewels. They competed in matches against other middle schoolers, answering tough questions about all kinds of subjects.

"Maybe," Jasmine said. "But Willow's captain." She lowered her voice. "And she makes all the decisions about the jewel stuff, too."

"Now, you know that's not fair," Willow said. "We make decisions together. Anyway, if I was doing everything, like you say, then why are *you* the one who's holding on to the diamond?"

"Hey, keep it down," Erin warned, looking around. The diamond Willow was talking about was technically stolen.

"It's because I collect gems and I know a lot about them," Jasmine answered in a loud whisper. "Like how to keep them safe."

"Oh, really?" Willow asked. "So where is it?"

"In my locker, of course," Jasmine said.

Willow, Erin, and Lili stopped in their tracks.

"Jasmine, are you serious?" Lili asked. "That doesn't seem like a safe place at all."

"Of course it is," Jasmine explained. "My locker has a lock on it. And I hid it really well, in a secret box behind my locker mirror."

Willow shook her head. "That's the worst idea ever. You know the Rivals are dying to get that diamond. They can walk into this school any time they want, and our lockers are the first place they would look."

The Rivals, the quiz bowl team from Atkinson Preparatory School, had stolen the diamond in the first place. And they would stop at nothing to get it back.

"She's right," Erin agreed. "We need a better hiding place for it."

Jasmine looked hurt. "See what I mean? Willow says something, and everyone just automatically agrees with her."

"Let's meet after school and talk about it," Lili suggested, suddenly very uncomfortable with the way her friends were fighting. "In the library. We can all vote on where to hide it, and then everyone will have a say. Okay?"

Jasmine and Willow eyed each other.

"Okay," Willow said, her dark brown eyes flashing with determination.

"Fine," agreed Jasmine.

"Thank goodness," Erin said. "Now let's get changed!"

A few hours later, Erin and Lili got to the library first and found a table. Jasmine and Willow walked through the door at the same time, but neither one of them was smiling.

"We've got to do something," Lili whispered to Erin. "I hate it when people are mad at each other."

"Let's just talk about the jewels," Erin replied. "Once we get talking, things will get back to normal."

Willow and Jasmine each took a seat.

"So, let's discuss the diamond," Erin said right away. "I was thinking that we should, um, write down a list of everything that's happened so far. You know, to figure out what to do next."

Willow looked impressed. "I was thinking the same thing," she said.

The girls reached into their backpacks, and each one retrieved a big green pen shaped like the Statue of Liberty. They all glanced at each other and laughed.

"We look like the Statue of Liberty fan club," Erin joked.

"They are pretty ridiculous," Willow admitted.

"I love mine!" Lili said, pressing a button on the pen. Tiny green bulbs lit up the statue's crown. "Now I can write in the dark!"

"I like it because it reminds me of our trip to New York," Jasmine said, with a dreamy look in her eyes. "I would love to live there someday."

A few weeks before, the girls had traveled to New York City for a regional quiz bowl tournament. Since they'd returned, the Jewels had been busy entering more quiz bowl matches so they could earn points to qualify for the national tournament later that spring. And when they weren't doing homework, studying for quiz bowl, or babysitting little brothers, they tried to find out what they could about a mystery they'd uncovered: the secret of the four Martha Washington jewels.

"New York was awesome, but things have been pretty slow since then, jewel-wise," Erin pointed out. "I think we need to start taking action!"

Willow waved her pen. "I agree! Let's start with our notes. First, the Rivals stole the ruby from our school. We figured it out but nobody believed us. They hid it in a museum and we tried to get it back, but they beat us to it."

"Right," Erin said, busily writing. "And then —"

"And then," Jasmine interrupted, "Erin found an old letter from Martha Washington talking about four jewels that hold a secret together: a ruby, a diamond, an emerald, and a sapphire. And she also found a diary of Martha's where it says the jewels hold clues."

Willow nodded. "But before Erin found that in the diary, Lili discovered a note in her coat pocket that told us the Rivals were planning to steal the diamond in New York. Then on the train we got another message telling us to meet at the Alice statue in Central Park. And *that* message told us we were looking in the wrong place."

"Right!" Jasmine agreed. "So we figured out that the diamond was hidden in a desk at the Metropolitan Museum of Art. And then we got another message, a map that showed how the Rivals were planning to steal the diamond. But we tricked them and stole it for ourselves."

Erin grinned. "Yeah, that was fun."

"And then Jasmine took the diamond out of its setting, and we found a clue etched in the back," Lili said. "E-Fifty."

Jasmine jotted down some notes. "So that's what happened in New York. Since then, I've been researching emeralds and sapphires from Martha Washington's era to try and find out which gems the Rivals might be after next."

"And how's that going?" Lili asked.

Jasmine sighed. "I've been doing Internet research and taking out every single book from the school library that could help," she said.

"But it's like looking for a needle in a haystack. We need a clue or something — anything! — to narrow it down."

"Lili and I have been scouring the library, too, hoping we could find another letter or something else written by Martha to point us in the right direction," Erin said.

"But so far, no luck." Lili frowned.

Willow nodded. "I've been doing some research, too, to try and figure out what the E-Fifty on the back of the diamond could mean. It could be part of a math equation. Also, there is a World War Two tank that has a model number E-Fifty, as well as a smartphone. But those are way after Martha's time, so I ruled them out. I'm thinking the E-Fifty will make sense once we see the clues on the other jewels."

"*If* we see the clues on the other jewels," Jasmine pointed out. "The Rivals definitely have the ruby. For all we know, they might have already stolen the emerald and sapphire, too."

All of a sudden Erin nudged Jasmine. "*Shhh!* Here comes Principal Frederickson!"

A stern-looking African-American woman marched into the library. Principal Frederickson always walked like she knew exactly where she was going. Today, she was headed right for the girls' table.

The Jewels quickly stopped talking and closed their notebooks.

Erin greeted her in her most polite voice. "Hello, Principal Frederickson."

Their principal raised an eyebrow, and Erin swore she saw something resembling a twinkle in her eyes.

"You don't have to hide anything from me, girls," she said. Then she leaned forward, placing her hands on the table. "I know what you're doing. And I know all about the Martha Washington jewels."

Chapter Two

The girls were too stunned to speak.

"I think we should continue this conversation in my office," the principal said, and the girls immediately stood up and followed her out of the library. Curious classmates gazed at them as they walked away. Their eyes seemed to wonder if the Jewels were in trouble.

If only they really knew, Jasmine thought, avoiding their stares. After the ruby had been stolen, Principal Frederickson told the girls to forget about it and concentrate on quiz bowl instead. They sure hadn't done as she'd asked. In fact, they'd only gotten more involved. *If she knows about the diamond, too, we're in big trouble!*

Erin, on the other hand, was excited. *Maybe Principal Frederickson knows the secret of the four jewels*, she thought hopefully.

But all of the girls kept their fears and questions to themselves until they were settled in the principal's office. Principal Frederickson sat behind her gleaming wood desk, and the girls took seats facing her.

"So, how do you know about the jewels?" Erin blurted out. The suspense was too much for her.

"As you know, I was also a student at Martha Washington School," she said. "Back then, there was a rumor going around that Martha Washington had hidden four special jewels somewhere. Nobody knew where, or why the jewels were important. The story intrigued me, so I looked through some books in the library. But my research didn't get me very far, and I eventually gave up on it. When I left the school, I concentrated on college and my career — but the story has always stayed in the back of my mind."

"And then the Martha Washington ruby got stolen," Jasmine said, jumping in.

Principal Frederickson nodded. "Yes. I had always suspected it was one of the four special jewels. And when you girls told me you had proof that the Rivals took it, I wasn't sure what to think — until Arthur Atkinson made that spectacle on the news."

After a private phone call from Principal Frederickson, the director of Atkinson Prep, Arthur Atkinson, had alerted the news. He accused the Jewels of trying to throw suspicion on the Rivals just so they would have a quiz bowl advantage. It was humiliating for all of the girls.

"That was terrible," Jasmine remembered with a shudder.

"Well, that's when I began to suspect that the Rivals really were behind the theft," Principal Frederickson said, "and that maybe Arthur Atkinson knew something about the secret of the four jewels. So I started researching again. That's when I noticed that someone was taking lots of Martha Washington books out from the library."

She looked directly at Erin, and a red flush spread across Erin's freckles.

"I thought maybe the books would help us figure stuff out," Erin explained. "And then I read Martha Washington's diary, and . . ."

"I found the diary in the library and put it in your pile of books," Principal Frederickson admitted. "I thought you girls were having fun with the story, just like I had when I was your age."

Willow got a spark in her eyes. "Wait a second! Are you the one who sent us those messages? The ones on yellow paper?"

Principal Frederickson looked concerned. "No, I did not. What kind of messages?"

"Before we went to New York, I found a message in my coat pocket that said that the Rivals were going to steal the diamond," Lili said.

"And then we found more notes that helped us find the diamond," Willow added.

Now it was Principal Frederickson's turn to look stunned.

"You found the diamond?" she asked, standing up.

"Well, we figured out that it was hidden in this desk in the Metropolitan Museum of Art," Erin explained. "And Ryan from the Rivals stole it, but we tricked him. He thought he was handing it off to Isabel, but he handed it to me instead. And then I handed it to Willow, and she ran really fast —"

"You *stole* from the Metropolitan Museum of Art?!" Principal Frederickson gasped in shock. "Do your parents know about this?"

"No, but we didn't actually *steal* anything," Erin insisted. "The Rivals did. And, besides, the museum doesn't even know the diamond exists."

"And when we accused the Rivals of stealing before, nobody believed us," Jasmine pointed out.

Principal Frederickson shook her head. "This is precisely why I wanted to talk to you today. I noticed that you've been doing a lot more research on the jewels, and I thought things might have gone too far." She nervously paced back and forth across the floor. "I can see I was right. Where is the diamond now?"

"In my locker," Jasmine piped up.

The principal stopped in her tracks. She looked right at Jasmine.

"In . . . your . . . locker?" she asked in disbelief.

"Told you it was a bad idea," Willow muttered.

"I'll go get it," Jasmine offered quickly.

"Yes," Principal Frederickson said. "Please do that."

Jasmine got up and raced off. She returned a few minutes later, her heart pounding. She handed a small black box to Principal Frederickson.

Their principal opened the lid to reveal a pair of diamond earrings. One of them had been taken out of its setting by Jasmine, back in New York.

"There's a clue etched on the back of that one," Erin said, leaning over the desk to point at the loose diamond. "E-Fifty. But we're not sure what it means."

The principal slowly sat back into her chair. "Amazing," she said. "But how did you know where to find the diamond?"

"It was something Erin found in the diary," Willow replied, and then she explained how the girls had tracked down the desk that had been built by a Quaker friend of Martha Washington's.

Principal Frederickson nodded. "That's brilliant. I know you girls are very smart. But I had no idea you would be so successful. I'm not sure I would have given you the diary if I'd known you'd be semi-accomplices to a national museum heist."

Jasmine felt flattered, but confused. "So are we in trouble?"

Principal Frederickson shook her head. "No, but I'm not happy about this. Things could have gone wrong. *Very* wrong. What if one of you had gotten hurt? I understand your motives were good. But, you should have told me about the diamond as soon as you got back from New York," she said sternly. "And now, I want to make this very clear: You girls will stay out of this from now on. If Arthur Atkinson wants this diamond, he'll do anything to get it. This started out as fun, but I'm afraid it's getting dangerous."

"But we can't stop now!" Erin protested. "The Rivals still have the ruby. And we don't know if they have the emerald or the sapphire, or if those jewels are still out there somewhere."

"I appreciate your passion, girls. Martha Washington would have been proud of you," Principal Frederickson said. "But I really think you need to step back and let me handle this from now on. I have my own suspicions about the emerald and the sapphire. And I think you should let me have the diamond for safekeeping."

"Of course," Willow said quickly, but Jasmine shot her an accusatory look.

"We should all discuss it," Jasmine broke in. "After all, we found it together."

"But Principal Frederickson can keep it safe for us," Willow said. "It's the best thing to do."

"I agree," Erin said. "But maybe Principal Frederickson could let us know if any interesting stuff happens. Like if she finds out what the clues mean. What do you think, Lili?"

"Sounds good to me," Lili said.

The girls looked at Jasmine.

"That's fine," she said with a sigh. "If Principal Frederickson agrees."

"Of course," the principal said. "That's only fair. I imagine you must all be very curious to know what the jewels mean. But it's too dangerous for you to hold the diamond. I promise to keep it safe for you. Now, I'm afraid I've kept you long enough."

"Thank you," Willow said, standing up. Jasmine took one last, longing look at the diamond before the Jewels left the principal's office.

"I still can't believe it," Erin said when they were out in the hallway. "Principal Frederickson knew about the jewels all along!"

Jasmine let out a dramatic sigh. "I guess our days of jewel hunting are over!"

Chapter Three

"Well, I, for one, am glad she knows," Willow said. "After all, the Rivals have had Arthur Atkinson helping them this whole time."

"We did okay without our principal helping us," Jasmine pointed out. "We got the diamond, after all."

Erin stopped short. "I just thought of something! What if Principal Frederickson is, like, an evil spy or something? Or a double agent? Maybe she's going to give the diamond right to Arthur Atkinson!"

"She wouldn't do that," Willow insisted.

"I don't know," Lili said. "She did call Arthur Atkinson after we told her about the Rivals stealing the ruby."

"Exactly," Willow said. "And he betrayed her by going on the news. So they couldn't be working together."

Everyone was quiet for a minute.

"Well, it's out of our hands now," Willow said. "We need to concentrate on quiz bowl, anyway. We've got a big match coming up."

"Right," Jasmine agreed. "We've got practice tomorrow. We really need to prepare."

The Jewels met for practice after school on Friday in Ms. Keatley's room. The history teacher was also their official quiz bowl advisor.

"Okay, we're going to do some drills today," Ms. Keatley announced at the start of practice. Her blond hair was pulled back into a messy ponytail, as usual.

"Erin," she said. "Name the first ten US presidents, please."

Erin wrinkled up her nose, thinking. "George Washington, Thomas Jefferson, John Adams, James Madison, James Monroe, John *Quincy* Adams, Andrew Jackson, Martin van Buren, William Henry Harrison, and . . . John Tyler!" she said triumphantly.

"Correct!" said Ms. Keatley. "Okay, Lili. How about five books written by Charles Dickens?"

"Um, *A Christmas Carol*, definitely," she said thoughtfully, counting on her fingers. "And *David Copperfield*, and *Oliver Twist*, *A Tale of Two Cities*, and *Great Expectations*."

"Very good," said the teacher. "Except the full title is *The Adventures of Oliver Twist*. Small details like that can make the difference between winning and losing points."

"Got it," Lili said earnestly. "I hate losing points for an incomplete answer! It's so painful, isn't it?"

"Definitely," agreed Jasmine. "But we haven't had a lot of wrong answers lately. We're doing pretty great."

"But we still need to practice," Willow pointed out. "I'm ready, Ms. Keatley. Give me your toughest equations." They spent the next hour answering rapid-fire questions posed by Ms. Keatley. Each team member had an area she was best in. Erin took the history questions, Willow handled the math, Jasmine answered the science questions, and Lili managed the arts and literature sections.

"Nice work today, girls," Ms. Keatley said, standing up to stretch when they were done. "The meet tomorrow is here at Martha Washington. Be sure to arrive by ten."

Willow looked at the sports watch on her wrist. "Anyone want to go to the Java Hut before we get picked up?"

"Mmm, their caramel cocoa is the best," Erin said. "Count me in."

Just around the corner from Martha Washington School, the Java Hut was small enough to be cozy but large enough to hold the middle-school students and office workers who went there for coffee and baked treats every day. The girls got steaming cups of cocoa at the counter and found a table by the sunny front window.

"Spring is finally here," Lili said with a smile as she looked out the window. "Everything is starting to turn green."

"I can't wait for softball season," Willow said.

"I don't know . . . all this sunshine," Jasmine noted, frowning. "It's so . . . cheerful!"

Lili laughed. "Jasmine, I swear I am going to make you a T-shirt with rainbows all over it," she threatened. "And glitter paint!"

That made Jasmine laugh, too. She closed her eyes and stuck out her tongue. "Ack! Too much cuteness!"

Willow's expression turned serious. "Well, look who it is," she said with a nod toward the door.

The girls turned to see Ryan Atkinson and Isabel Baudin walk into the coffee shop. Ryan was captain of the Rivals, and Isabel, who'd moved to the DC area from France, was a member of the team.

"Hey, guys!" Willow said brightly, waving at them.

But Ryan and Isabel looked straight ahead, pretending that they didn't hear her. They walked up to the counter and ordered their drinks.

The girls leaned in to the table and started to talk in loud whispers.

"Weird," Erin said. "Isabel didn't even insult me."

"And Ryan didn't flash me that 'I'm better than you' smile," Willow pointed out.

"They sure are acting strange," Jasmine agreed. "We haven't seen them much since the New York trip. Only at a couple of quiz bowl meets. And they were acting like their usual obnoxious selves. So what gives today?"

Lili looked thoughtful. "And what are they doing here?" she wondered. "It's pretty far from Atkinson Prep."

"Maybe they came for the awesome cocoa," Erin suggested.

Jasmine frowned. "Or maybe they're here to scope out the school so they can steal back the diamond."

"Then they're out of luck," Lili said. "Principal Frederickson said she would keep it safe, and I believe her."

Ryan and Isabel got their drinks, then looked around at the tables. The only empty one was right next to the Jewels. The two Rivals whispered to each other for a moment and then headed for the front door.

"Good luck at the match tomorrow!" Erin called out.

Ryan stopped and turned around. "Thanks. You, too," he said gruffly. Isabel managed a glare in their direction, but that was about it. Then they left the shop.

"This is fantastic!" Willow said loudly, now that they no longer had to whisper. "Do you know what this means?"

"That Isabel has laryngitis?" Erin joked. "I mean, I've never seen her so quiet."

"Ha-ha," Willow said flatly. "No. It means that we have the psychological advantage tomorrow, for the first time ever."

Jasmine grinned. "Ooh, I like the sound of that."

Lili pointedly looked at Jasmine and Willow. "We'll only have an advantage if we stay strong as a team. You know what I mean. No more fighting! Or I'll have to sprinkle you with happy magical unicorn glitter before the match, and that takes *weeks* to get out of your hair."

Jasmine made a face at Lili. "I'll wear a hat."

"Seriously!" Lili said. "You guys have to promise me. No more arguing."

Jasmine and Willow looked at each other. Then they both smiled.

"Promise," Willow said.

"Me, too," agreed Jasmine.

Lili put her arms around both of them. "Yay!"

Erin rolled her eyes. "All right, enough. You guys are sweeter than my caramel cocoa. I'm having a sugar overload."

"I have a good feeling about this match tomorrow," Willow said. "Finally beating the Rivals? Now that would be *really* sweet!"

Chapter Four

The next morning dawned bright and sunny. The air was crisp but the spring sun worked hard to bring the temperature up into the sixties by the time Erin's mother brought the Jewels to Martha Washington School. They gathered in the auditorium as quiz bowl members from neighboring schools trickled in. Each girl wore a red T-shirt with the words "Jewels Rule!" on the front.

"I still feel like it makes us look like we're bragging," Willow said, gazing down at her shirt.

"What's wrong with bragging?" Erin asked, with a twinkle in her eye.

"I'm just glad we finally agreed on something," Jasmine said. "I think they came out great, Lili."

Lili beamed. "Thanks! Doing the lettering was easy once I made the stencil."

Erin's mother smiled. "Well, I think you all look fabulous. I'm going to sit in the 'Mom' section now. Break a leg, you guys."

Erin cringed. "I hate when you say that. It makes me nervous to walk up onstage."

Mrs. Fischer just smiled and gave her daughter a kiss. Then she walked off to get a seat in the center of the auditorium.

Ms. Keatley hurried up to them, holding a clipboard.

"Looks like you're up first, guys," she said. "Against the team from West Chatsworth. If you beat them, you'll have the chance to compete against the winner of the second match."

"Great!" Willow said. "We're feeling good today, Ms. Keatley. We won't let you down."

Ms. Keatley smiled. "You never do. You always do your best, and I'm proud of you whether you win or lose."

The sound of microphone feedback filled the auditorium, and the chattering quiz bowl contestants and guests quieted down. The moderator, a dark-haired woman in a gray suit, spoke into the mike. "Will the teams from Martha Washington and West Chatsworth please take the stage?"

The girls climbed onstage and took their places. A lectern with a microphone and buzzer was set up for every player on each team. As Willow adjusted her mike, she noticed Principal Frederickson sitting in the front row. The principal smiled at Willow and gave her a thumbs-up.

Willow nudged Jasmine, who always stood at the lectern next to hers. "Did you see that?" she asked.

Jasmine nodded. "It's nice that she's here, I guess. I just hope she doesn't make me nervous!"

"Contestants, please make sure your buzzers are working," the moderator instructed, and then she went on to explain the rules of the match, which the girls all knew by heart. The moderator would ask a series of toss-up questions worth ten points each. If the team got the question right, they could try to answer three bonus questions for extra points. If they got the question wrong, ten points were deducted from their score.

The moderator read the first question. "In 2011, Steven Spielberg directed this film based on the comic book series created by Belgian artist Georges Remi."

Lili buzzed in. "*Tin* — I mean, *The Adventures of Tintin*," she corrected herself quickly, remembering Ms. Keatley's advice.

"Correct," the moderator said, and Lili grinned at Ms. Keatley from the stage.

The training paid off for all of the girls, and the Jewels beat the team from West Chatsworth handily. When they got off the stage, Principal Frederickson approached them.

"Wonderful job, girls," she said. "You're a credit to Martha Washington School."

"Thanks," Willow said.

"Any news about the jewels?" Erin broke in eagerly.

A look of amusement flashed across Principal Frederickson's face.

"Seriously, Erin?" the principal asked. "You and your teammates just won a quiz bowl match and that is all you can think about?"

"Yep." Erin grinned. "Pretty much."

Principal Frederickson glanced at the people still in the auditorium. "Let's talk about this in the hallway."

The girls followed her out of the auditorium and into the empty corridor.

Principal Frederickson sighed. "There is something," she admitted reluctantly. "But I'm really not sure how much more you girls need to know. This is a very unusual situation, one I never imagined any of my students would get mixed up in."

The girls looked at one another. Principal Frederickson knew something! But how could they get her to share it?

"Oh, tell us, tell us!" Erin begged.

"Please?" Lili asked with her sweetest smile.

"We already know about the jewels," Willow reminded her.

Jasmine nodded. "So what's the harm in filling us in?"

"The cat's already out of the bag, isn't it?" Principal Frederickson asked with a rueful grin. "All right. I do have some news. It's about the emerald. Years ago, I figured out that the emerald Martha was talking about was purchased by a wealthy shipping family. Then I lost track of it. But I've seen it in the news recently."

"The news? Was it stolen?" Willow asked.

Principal Frederickson shook her head. "No. It's just getting a lot of publicity. Do you know who Derrica Girard is?"

"Ooh, she's that super-rich famous woman from TV," Lili said.

"*East Coast Class*, that show about wealthy housewives," Erin said, and Willow looked at her, surprised. Erin shrugged. "Mary Ellen watches it all the time. I can't help it if my big sister has terrible taste in television."

"Well, Derrica's been wearing the emerald everywhere, and I'm sure it's the same one," Principal Frederickson said. "I've been trying to get in touch with her, but it's difficult now that she's on TV."

Erin's eyes grew wide. "So that means the Rivals don't have the emerald!"

"And if you can get to Derrica first, you can ask to see it!" Jasmine sounded excited. "Maybe there is another clue on it."

"If you can get in touch with her, what will you tell her?" Willow asked.

"I'll tell her that her emerald is an important part of history, and I'll ask her if she will let me examine it," Principal Frederickson said.

"After all, we don't need the emerald to solve Martha's mystery. Just the clue etched on the back."

The girls were quiet as they considered this.

"That's awesome news," Erin said. "I hope she lets you look at it."

Though the Jewels were excited Principal Frederickson had a lead on the emerald, it was hard not to be a part of it. Willow broke the silence that had settled on the group.

"Hey, we'd better get back inside," she said. "I want to see the Rivals' match. Thanks for letting us know about the emerald, Principal Frederickson."

"You're welcome," she replied. "I should return to my seat, too, so I can watch your next turn. Good luck."

They headed back inside the auditorium, where the Rivals were taking the stage with the competing team, the Maryville Marvels. After a few questions, it was clear that the Rivals were off their game. In the end they won, but only after a nail-biting tiebreaker question.

"We'll take a short break," the moderator announced. "Then I need to see the Jewels and the Rivals back onstage."

Willow held out her arm to the other girls. "I think it's time for a cheer. Math!"

Jasmine slapped her hand on top of Willow's. "Science!"

Erin added her hand. "History!"

"Arts and Literature!" Lili cried with a giggle, slapping her hand on top of Erin's. "Mine is so long!"

Then the four girls raised their arms high in the air. "Goooo, Jewels!"

Their hearts were racing with excitement as they took the stage. Willow glanced over at the Rivals. Ryan was purposely ignoring her gaze, just like he had in the coffee shop. Normally, he'd be giving her a smug smile. Isabel looked sullen. Aaron Santiago, the third Rival, actually seemed nervous. Only Veronica Manasas, the fourth member of the team, looked as confident as ever. Her brown eyes were fixed on the moderator, and her hand was on top of the buzzer, ready to go.

"Your first question. Which of these numbers is *not* a prime number? Seven, thirty-seven, fifty-seven, or ninety-seven?"

There was a one-second pause, and then Willow and Ryan both hit their buzzers nearly at the same time.

"That goes to Martha Washington," the moderator said, and Willow grinned.

"Fifty-seven," she replied.

"Correct," said the moderator. "And now for your bonus questions."

The first question set the tone of the match. Ryan, Isabel, and Aaron just couldn't make it to the buzzer in time. Veronica, the team's science expert, started buzzing in on almost every question.

"By purpose, how is the following sentence classified?" the moderator began. "'I am going to the store.'"

Lili pressed on her buzzer, but Veronica beat her to it.

"It's a statement," Veronica answered.

"Correct," said the moderator, and the Rivals got three bonus questions.

When they got to the last toss-up question, the moderator announced, "Right now, the score is tied. The winner of this last toss-up will win the match."

Willow glanced over at the Rivals. Except for Veronica, they all seemed to be sweating. She looked at her teammates, who looked more confident and determined than she'd ever seen them.

"We can do this," she mouthed.

"And now the last question," the moderator began. "What is the name of the upper arm bone in a human?"

Veronica was right on the buzzer, but Jasmine was a split second faster.

"The humerus!" she practically yelled, as a lock of her curly hair fell across her eyes.

"Correct," the moderator said. "This match goes to the Martha Washington Jewels!"

The girls couldn't help it — they burst into excited shrieks and cheers. Willow was the first to remember the proper protocol.

"Hey, we've got to shake the Rivals' hands," she reminded them.

"Can you believe it?" Lili asked, smiling. "We finally beat the Rivals at quiz bowl!"

"Pinch me, I must be dreaming," Erin said. "I've thought about this moment so many times, how can I be sure it's real? Ouch!" she cried as Lili gave her a pinch on the arm.

"It *is* real. All that studying paid off," Jasmine said with a grin.

The girls calmed down and lined up to greet the Rivals.

"Good job," Ryan said, shaking Willow's hand, and he sounded sincere. Isabel didn't say anything at all. Aaron gave her a smile.

Then she got to Veronica.

"You almost had us," Willow said, looking her in the eye. She wanted to make sure Veronica got the message: Willow knew Veronica had carried her whole team that day.

To Willow's surprise, Veronica answered her.

"Thanks. It's because I actually care about quiz bowl," she said. "Not like some of my other team members."

Willow couldn't wait to tell the other girls about Veronica's comment. But when they got offstage, Erin tapped her on the shoulder and pointed to Principal Frederickson. She was on her cell phone, looking very upset.

Erin ran up to her principal. "Is everything okay?"

"The security company just notified me that the alarm in my office has been activated," she said. "The police are on their way."

"Oh no!" Erin cried. "You don't think —"

Principal Frederickson nodded. "That's what I'm afraid of."

She hurried out of the auditorium, and Erin motioned for the other girls to follow them. They ran to Principal Frederickson's office. The door was open. The principal raced behind her desk, to a painting on the wall. But while the left side of the painting was connected to the wall, the rest of it swung out — like an open door. The girls quickly realized that the painting was actually the door to a safe.

Principal Frederickson opened the door all the way.

"It's gone," she said in a defeated voice. "The diamond has been stolen!"

Chapter Five

Jasmine gasped. Lili and Erin stood with their mouths open while Willow peered inside the safe.

"It *is* gone," Willow said sadly. "I guess it would have been safer in Jasmine's locker after all!"

Jasmine sighed heavily. *Not another stolen gem*, she thought unhappily. The prospect of failure, even just moments after beating the Rivals at quiz bowl, was unbearable.

Erin looked at her friend with raised eyebrows and, placing a hand in front of her face, gestured toward Principal Frederickson. "Double agent," Erin mouthed silently.

"Erin, I can see you," Principal Frederickson said as Erin, startled, put her hand down and stood up straight. "I assure you, I am no double agent. But the timing is suspicious. Who would have known I had the diamond in my possession? Did you girls tell anyone?"

All of the Jewels vigorously shook their heads. "No way!" Erin cried.

Jasmine and Willow also responded with a no, but Lili hung her head sheepishly. "I did tell Eli," she admitted. Lili's brother, Eli, a high school student at Atkinson Prep, was a computer genius. His tech savvy had helped the girls keep the diamond out of the Rivals' hands — so far.

Lili quickly explained to Principal Frederickson how Eli had been aiding them.

"He has kept everything a secret. I know he wouldn't have said a word to anyone," Lili said passionately. She might argue with her brother from time to time, but she trusted him completely.

The other Jewels did, too. "As far as I'm concerned, Eli is an honorary Jewel and totally trustworthy," Willow said firmly. Erin and Jasmine nodded in agreement.

Principal Frederickson listened closely before commenting. "From everything you've told me, I agree."

"It has to be the Rivals, right?" Jasmine asked. "We saw them at Java Hut yesterday afternoon. They were probably making plans to steal the diamond!"

"Of course it was the Rivals!" Erin fumed. "And they're still on campus. Let's go get them!" She started to run out of the office, but Principal Frederickson gently placed a hand on her shoulder.

"Not so fast," she said. "The alarm was tripped at ten fifty-one a.m. The Rivals were onstage competing against all of you at that exact moment. I know. I was in the audience watching when the call came in from the security company. No one left the stage at any time during the quiz bowl match."

Two uniformed police officers walked into the room. As Principal Frederickson moved to join them she turned to the Jewels and said, "Girls, if you would please excuse us?"

The girls walked out into the hall. Actually, Erin stomped. She was furious.

"Those rotten, no-good thieves!" she said. "This is the second time they've waltzed into our school and stolen a gem right from under our noses. First the ruby, now the diamond."

As Erin slumped against the wall in frustration, Willow wondered aloud, "But how could it be the Rivals? You heard Principal Frederickson. They were onstage — *with us* — when the alarm went off."

"We're the Rivals' alibi!" Lili sounded shocked at her own conclusion. "Who would have ever imagined that?"

"Wait," Jasmine said. "What if they used something to trigger the alarm after they had already stolen the diamond? Maybe they stole it *before* the quiz bowl."

Willow nodded. "It's a possibility. We know Arthur Atkinson is helping them, so who knows what kind of gadgets he's providing?"

Before they could explore the idea any further, the police walked out of Principal Frederickson's office.

"I'm so sorry about that, officers," Principal Frederickson said smoothly. "There must have been some kind of malfunction with the alarm. I will let the security company know."

"Hey!" Erin cried. "There is no problem with the —"

A warning glance from Principal Frederickson stopped Erin from saying anything else.

"I mean, bye, have a nice day," Erin said awkwardly. "Thanks for, um, protecting and serving, and all that good stuff."

The officers gave a polite nod before leaving.

"Why didn't you tell them?" Erin asked in disbelief after the police officers had left.

"Come inside my office. We'll talk in here." Principal Frederickson held the door open as the girls passed her and filed inside the room. She shut the door tightly behind her before sitting down at her desk.

"Now, girls, I could not report something as stolen that I wasn't even supposed to have possession of in the first place, now could I?" she asked. "What if they wanted to know where the diamond came from?"

Jasmine's eyes narrowed. "I bet the Rivals were counting on the fact that we couldn't report it."

Principal Frederickson nodded. "I think you are right about that, Jasmine."

Willow looked deep in thought. "We had an idea while we were in the hall. Maybe the Rivals stole the diamond before the meet and did something else to trigger the alarm while they were onstage with us, giving them the perfect alibi."

Jasmine flashed an angry look at Willow. That had been her idea!

"It's a possibility. But I know how we can find out for sure," Principal Frederickson answered as she switched on her computer. "We'll take a look at the security footage." As the girls eagerly gathered around, she clicked on the System Defender program on her desktop. The security software launched, showing a live video of the office. Erin waved at the camera and stuck her tongue out, while the others laughed.

"Pretty cool program," Lili admired.

"It lets me monitor my office security camera from any computer, even my smartphone," Principal Frederickson explained. "It's part of the school's campus-wide security system. Now let's see," she said as she clicked and the live feed began to rewind. "First we will go back to right before ten fifty-one, when the alarm was triggered."

The video footage at 10:50 showed an empty office, with no signs of activity. Everyone watched quietly. At 10:51 a.m., a man entered the room, pushing a janitor's cart. He was short, and he wore the button-down navy work shirt that all the custodians at Martha Washington used. But instead of emptying the trash can or vacuuming, he went straight for the picture behind Principal Frederickson's desk, swinging open the false-painted cover and revealing the locked safe door.

From his tool belt he pulled out a small, slim device and held it to the top corner of the safe door. A low, whirring sound could be heard on the audio. After a few seconds, he put what seemed to be a drill back in his tool belt and pulled out a different instrument. This one had a piece of long, flexible tubing that he inserted into the hole he had just drilled. He threaded it through until it disappeared, then looked into the eyepiece at the end. Then he reached a hand to the combination dial and began to turn it slowly. After a few moments, he stopped and pulled the tubing out of the safe. He opened the safe door and grabbed the small black box that held the diamond earrings. He opened it quickly to check the contents before placing it in his shirt pocket. After glancing at his watch, he quickly wheeled the janitor cart out of the room, leaving the door of the safe ajar.

"So the diamond *was* stolen while both you and the Rivals were competing onstage," Principal Frederickson said thoughtfully.

"But who could have taken it?" Lili wondered. "He doesn't look like any of the custodians that work here."

"He most certainly does not," Principal Frederickson said. "I would know."

"There is something really familiar about him, though," Willow remarked. "Is there any way to zoom in on his face?"

"I was just about to suggest that myself," the principal answered. She rewound the footage and found a spot where the thief's face was turned toward the camera. With a few clicks, she zoomed in.

Willow nodded. "I knew he looked familiar. That's Aaron Santiago in disguise!"

Chapter Six

"Whoa! Wait just a second. How is that possible?" Erin questioned. "According to the time stamp on the video, the theft started at ten fifty-one a.m. The exact moment we were beating the Rivals onstage in front of a roomful of people!"

"And Aaron was there the entire time, I am positive of that," Principal Frederickson replied.

"Are you sure that's Aaron?" Jasmine squinted at the screen.

"It's him, I just know it!" Willow insisted. "And we all know how he likes to put on disguises. Remember his security guard getup at the Smithsonian? Or how about his old lady costume at the Metropolitan Museum of Art?"

Principal Frederickson raised an eyebrow. "Really?" she asked.

"That's true." Lili nodded. "He does have a flair for the dramatic."

"Yes, but is Aaron also a master safecracker?" Jasmine wondered. "The thief on this video really knows his stuff. He got into that safe in a matter of minutes."

"Let's bring him in for questioning," Erin said. "We'll sit him down and shine a bright light in his eyes. Trust me; I've seen this in lots of TV shows. I'll be the bad cop. Lili can be the good cop. We'll have him confessing he believes in unicorns by the time we're done with him!"

Principal Frederickson shook her head. "Erin, you will do no such thing. Thank you for your help, girls, but I will take it from here."

"What?!" Erin asked, shocked. "Are you firing us?"

Principal Frederickson smiled kindly at her. "I don't think I ever hired you." But her smile turned to a frown. "You've done great work so far, and I'm very impressed with what you all are capable of. But let me remind you of our discussion. You are minors and, as students in this school, under my care. I absolutely do not want you girls in any danger. I will handle this."

"But —" Willow began.

"No buts," Principal Frederickson said firmly. "I'm afraid the matter is closed, girls. Thanks again for your help, and congratulations on your quiz bowl victory. You should be very proud of yourselves."

The girls exchanged glances. They knew it was no use arguing.

"Thank you," Willow said. "Please let us know if you need more help."

Principal Frederickson smiled. "I'm sure I'll be fine."

The other girls mumbled their thanks and followed Willow out of the principal's office.

Once in the hallway, they huddled into a circle. "We all heard Principal Frederickson," Willow said.

"Loud and clear," Erin replied glumly.

"We'll have to do what she says," Willow conceded. "But I'm going to keep my eyes and ears open just in case — and I suggest you all do the same. If we find out something useful, we can let Principal Frederickson know."

"We'll need to do more than that!" Jasmine cried. "Now the Rivals have the ruby AND the diamond. If the ruby has a clue on it, too, that means the Rivals are one step closer to learning the secret of the jewels."

"But what can we do?" Lili wondered.

Before anyone could answer her, a voice interrupted them.

"There you are!" Ms. Keatley said as she came hurrying down the hallway. "I've been looking everywhere for you. Congratulations!"

The girls gazed at one another with sad faces. Finally beating the Rivals in a quiz bowl match would normally have them grinning from ear to ear. But the stolen diamond had soured their victory. They managed to muster some smiles for Ms. Keatley's sake.

"I know you and the Rivals have been very competitive, but I also know how you tried to make friends with them on the New York trip," Ms. Keatley said. Erin stifled a cough while Willow flashed her a warning look. On the trip, the Jewels had convinced Ms. Keatley to arrange some outings with the Rivals in order to keep an eye on them, not because they enjoyed spending time together!

"Anyway," Ms. Keatley continued, "Josh thought we should take both teams out after the competition to celebrate. We're all going bowling!"

Josh Haverford was the Rivals' advisor. He had a huge crush on Ms. Keatley. But apparently she was the only one who couldn't tell. Even the Rivals were on to him. It had started in New York, when Mr. Haverford kept trying to make up reasons to be in the same place as Ms. Keatley and the Jewels. Since then, he always made sure to sit next to her at quiz bowl tournaments.

"Bowling?" Erin asked as she stifled a groan.

"Yes, and I got the okay from your parents. So as soon as quiz bowl is done for the day, we'll get going." Ms. Keatley beamed. She thought she was delivering great news.

"Um, hurray?" Lili said halfheartedly.

At the bowling alley, they reluctantly followed Ms. Keatley inside. Lois's Lanes was Hallytown's only bowling alley and a popular spot.

On a Saturday afternoon the place was crowded, but Mr. Haverford had arrived early and had a lane reserved for them.

"Over here!" he said as he waved an arm in the air, a smile spreading across his face.

"We'll be right there!" Ms. Keatley called. She turned to the girls. "We need to get our shoes first."

As they waited in line to rent their shoes, Willow looked around the bowling alley. The gleaming lanes reflected the colorful backdrops painted on the back wall above the pins. A café with seating that overlooked the lanes sold hot dogs, pizza, and other snacks. Willow watched Aaron, Ryan, and Isabel eating pizza together, talking and laughing. They seemed pretty happy considering they had just lost a quiz bowl match.

If they stole the diamond from us, they would *be celebrating,* she thought.

Veronica was down near the lane, sitting next to Mr. Haverford, her shoulders slumped. She was the only member of the Rivals who didn't look cheerful.

"These are such a fashion disaster," Lili said as she put her shoes on. "And you know how I love taking practically anything and turning it into a wearable work of art, but even I can't get inspired over these shoes."

"What are you talking about? Strike a pose!" Erin did a model spin in her shoes as everyone laughed.

By now, Aaron, Ryan, and Isabel had finished their pizza and were waiting with Mr. Haverford and Veronica. The teacher's smile grew even bigger when he saw Ms. Keatley.

"I've got to warn you, I am the king of gutter balls," he said with a laugh.

Behind Mr. Haverford's back, Ryan rolled his eyes. He caught Willow watching him and gave her his usual smug smile, the one he seemed to have misplaced at the Java Hut yesterday.

"I'm not much of a bowler, either," Ms. Keatley admitted with a smile.

"Don't worry, it's just for fun," Mr. Haverford assured her. "We've done our competing for the day. And congratulations, girls, on your wins!"

Mr. Haverford smiled again. He seemed really nice. *Way too nice to be the Rivals' advisor*, Jasmine thought.

Isabel gave a tiny, slightly mocking laugh. "Yes, congratulations," she said. "You win some, you lose some. That's how I like to think of it."

Erin felt her cheeks getting red. She just knew Isabel was talking about the diamond!

"Let's get started!" Mr. Haverford said cheerfully, ignoring — or most likely not noticing — the tension between Isabel and Erin.

They began to play. Willow was surprised at how well the Rivals bowled. Aaron did a funny series of silly steps before throwing his ball, but it worked. He scored a strike.

"Yes!" he said, smiling, as he high-fived Ryan.

Willow confidently took her turn and also had a strike.

Isabel daintily clutched the ball, then took a few tiny steps before throwing. She, too, threw a strike.

Erin watched her with an open mouth.

"What?" Isabel asked when she noticed Erin's shocked expression. Then she shrugged. "It's what passes for culture around here. My options are limited."

After Jasmine bowled, she noticed that Veronica still looked upset.

"Hey, are you okay?" Jasmine asked as she sat down beside her.

Veronica sighed. "I'm just bummed about losing today. Quiz bowl is really important to me, and I want to win."

"I totally understand that. We work so hard, studying and everything," Jasmine said. "But you can't win them all."

Veronica frowned. "I know that, but it's *why* we didn't win that bothers me. I only care about quiz bowl. Not this other stuff."

The "other stuff"? Jasmine wondered. Could Veronica mean the jewel thefts? It was strange. While the cat-and-mouse game between the Rivals and the Jewels continued, neither group had ever really talked about it to the other. Maybe Veronica knew how Aaron had gotten into the safe. Jasmine felt her heart race. Should she ask her? Before she could muster the courage, it was Veronica's turn to bowl.

The rest of the game went quickly. Jasmine didn't get a chance to talk to Veronica alone again, even though she was ready to ask some tough questions.

"Snack attack!" Erin called. "The smell of cheesy nachos is driving me to distraction. Does anyone else want something?"

"I'll share some nachos with you, Erin," Lili chimed in. "And don't forget some soda, too."

Erin went off for the snacks while Lili took her last turn. It was the final frame, and the score was close. If Lili kept bowling the way she had been, the Jewels would be the winners.

As Lili was lining up her shot, Erin came back with a tray loaded with food and drinks.

"I thought you were just getting nachos?" Willow asked.

"Everything looked so good, I couldn't decide," Erin said. "So I got a little bit of everything. We can share — whoa!"

As Erin stepped behind Lili, she started to lose her balance. The heavy tray wobbled in her hands.

"It's okay, I've got it!" Erin cried. "Wait a sec, maybe I don't!" she yelled as she fell, the tray flying up into the air.

She crashed into Lili just as Lili was about to bowl. The ball flew out of Lili's hands and went straight into the gutter. Both Lili and Erin crashed to the floor, the tray landing next to them as a shower of nachos, hot dogs, chicken strips, and French fries rained down on their heads.

"We won!" Isabel cheered.

Erin looked up. Her head was covered in nacho cheese. Lili sighed as she wrung out her shirt, which was now soaked in soda.

"Oh my goodness, are you okay?" Ms. Keatley asked. She helped the girls up and checked them for injuries while Aaron and Ryan laughed. Isabel pulled out her phone and snapped a photo of the fiasco.

Erin grabbed a strand of her cheese-covered hair and stuck it in her mouth. "I'm fine, but I'm still hungry!"

"Don't di-SPARE — we'll get you cleaned up," Mr. Haverford said with a chuckle at his bowling pun.

Willow groaned. "I think it's time to SPLIT!"

Chapter Seven

The next day, Willow sat at her desk in her bedroom finishing a book report that was due the next week. She had her door closed. Being the big sister to three little brothers sometimes required locking herself in her room in order to concentrate on her homework. Otherwise Alex, Michael, and Jason would never stop interrupting her.

She hummed along to the radio as she typed. A little background music always helped her to think. Her phone let out a beep, breaking her concentration. She picked it up to read a text from Erin:

Check out Isabel's Chatter page status. She's bragging about beating us in bowling! Even worse — she posted the photo!

Willow shook her head. Yesterday had started out so great — with the Jewels beating the Rivals at quiz bowl. Then the diamond went missing, and it all ended in a total disaster with the mishap at the bowling alley.

She quickly logged in to her Chatter account and went straight to Isabel's page. Sure enough, Isabel's status said: *Best day ever. Beat the Jewels at bowling. Have the pics to prove it!*

Underneath her status was a photo of Erin and Lili collapsed on the bowling lane, covered in food and soda. Isabel managed to get the scoreboard into the photo, too, showing the final score. Underneath the photo, Ryan had posted a smiley face as a comment.

Wow, Willow thought. *That's so totally obnoxious.*

She navigated to Ryan's page, curious to see if he was bragging, too. But he hadn't posted anything since the week before. Veronica's last update was Friday, the day prior to the quiz bowl meet. She had posted a link to a popular online quiz bowl study site, with a reminder for her teammates to study.

At least they're not all *being jerks*, Willow thought before checking out Aaron's page. Aaron had posted something only a few minutes ago. It was a video of his dog, an adorable black-and-white border collie, doing a trick. Aaron twirled his fingers in the air, and the dog spun in circles like it was chasing its tail. Aaron praised the dog and gave it a treat before the video ended. *Okay, so at least he* has a heart.

She browsed his page a little bit more when something caught her eye under the "Family" section. He listed a brother named Logan.

The photo looked a lot like Aaron. Willow didn't know he had a brother. Curious, she clicked on Logan's account. Logan had lots of friends, and they all seemed to go to Hallytown Middle School — not Atkinson.

I guess Aaron and Logan go to different schools, Willow considered as she clicked on Logan's photos. As she looked through them, she spotted one that was captioned "Me and my bro." Aaron and Logan stood side by side. Although they wore different clothes, Willow couldn't tell who was who. They were the same height and there was more than just a resemblance between them. Could they be twins?

Willow checked Logan's info. He listed his birthday as August 6. Next she looked at Aaron's birthday. It, too, was listed as August 6.

Willow grabbed her phone and started texting. The other Jewels needed to know about this — and fast!

"Thanks for getting online," Willow said to Jasmine, Lili, and Erin over her computer's microphone. Her friends' faces smiled at her from her computer screen. "We have to talk about this right away!"

"It's not every day that you call a webcam meeting," Jasmine said, giggling at how official that sounded. "I had to use my mom's computer to do this. Mine doesn't have a camera."

Lili waved. "Hello! So, what's the new info?"

Erin snorted. "Yeah. It's not exactly breaking news that Isabel is a jerk. She posted a photo of us covered in goo at the bowling alley on her Chatter account. And she's bragging about how she beat us at bowling."

Lili clicked her tongue. "She is so mean."

"Well, after Erin told me about that, I checked all of the Rivals' Chatter accounts," Willow explained. "I wanted to see if they were all badmouthing us. Turns out it was just Isabel. But I found something else that was pretty interesting."

Willow changed the view of her webcam to display her live computer screen instead of her face. On it was the photo of Aaron and his brother Logan.

"What the heck? Is that two Aarons?" Erin asked.

"Nope, it's Aaron and his brother — his *twin* brother," Willow said.

The girls were silent for a moment as they studied the photo.

"I didn't know Aaron had a twin brother," Lili said excitedly. "Do you know what this means?"

Willow switched her webcam view back to her own image. "I do. It means Logan could have been stealing the diamond while Aaron was competing. I knew that janitor looked like Aaron!"

Jasmine had her chin cupped in her hand. She was staring off into space.

"Earth to Jasmine!" Erin called.

Jasmine look startled. "Sorry, guys. I was lost in thought. After all the excitement at the bowling alley yesterday" — she was interrupted by Erin's groaning and Lili's giggling — "I forgot to tell you something strange Veronica said to me. She was really down in the dumps."

"I noticed," Willow said. "The way Isabel, Aaron, and Ryan were acting, you would have thought *they* won the quiz bowl match."

"Not Veronica. When I asked her what was wrong, she said it was WHY they didn't win that was upsetting her." Jasmine described the encounter. "She wasn't upset because they lost, she was bummed because of the reason why they lost."

"Why they lost," Lili repeated thoughtfully. "The Rivals really seemed off their game yesterday. I was able to pick up a lot of the art and history questions. Aaron was slow to hit the buzzer. And when he did, he got a couple of questions wrong. Which, for the Rivals, is, like, totally unheard of."

Erin snapped her fingers. "He even got that question about *Charlotte's Web* wrong. It wasn't like him."

"Maybe that's because it wasn't him," Jasmine said excitedly. "Maybe it was Logan instead!"

"And that's why Veronica was so upset," Willow chimed in. "Because she knew they were switching her experienced teammate with his brother!"

"I guess stealing the diamond was more important to them than winning the match," Jasmine said. "To all of them except Veronica. She was not a happy camper."

Erin smiled as a thought dawned on her. "So if Logan was onstage, pretending to be Aaron —"

"That left Aaron free to dress up like a janitor and steal the diamond!" Lili cried.

"I knew those no-good Rivals stole the diamond!" Erin shouted. "Why do they even bother trying to fool us? We're just too smart for them."

Willow grinned. "We've got to tell Principal Frederickson about this first thing tomorrow morning!"

Chapter Eight

The girls met at school fifteen minutes early the next morning. They went right to Principal Frederickson's office.

"Good morning, Jewels," Ms. Ortiz, the school secretary, said with a smile. "I heard about your win on Saturday. Congratulations!"

"Thanks," Willow replied. "Can we please talk to Principal Frederickson? It's about quiz bowl."

Ms. Ortiz hit the intercom. "The Jewels are here to see you."

"Let them in," came the principal's reply.

Principal Frederickson looked surprised to see the girls.

"Is everything all right?" she asked.

"We figured out something," Willow said excitedly. "Aaron Santiago has an identical twin brother! We think Logan was competing in the match while Aaron was stealing the diamond."

"That would certainly explain things," Principal Frederickson said thoughtfully. But then she got a stern look on her face. "I thought I told you girls to stop being detectives."

"We weren't out detecting or anything," Erin protested. "Willow was just looking online and found it. It fell right into our laps!"

"We thought you'd want to know," Willow added.

The principal eyed each of them carefully. "You're right. I'm glad you told me," she said. "However, I certainly hope nothing else *falls into your laps* regarding the jewels." She looked right at Erin.

Erin held up her right hand. "We promise."

Principal Frederickson nodded. "Good. Now please get to class. Have a good day, girls."

Jasmine shuddered when they got to the hallway.

"She is so scary when she's about to get mad," Jasmine said.

"I know," Lili agreed. "She reminds me of the Dragon Queen in the *Ice Odyssey* video game."

"She's being unfair," Erin protested. "We never asked to be involved in all this. But the Rivals dragged us in. I can't just step back."

"Me neither," Willow said. "But I think we have to."

At lunch that day, the girls sat together at their usual table. Lili was sketching in a notebook with her Statue of Liberty pen, and Erin absently poked at her salad with a fork.

"I've been thinking," she said. "How did the Rivals know where the diamond was?"

Jasmine looked around nervously. "Erin, we shouldn't even be talking about this."

"I'm not detecting," Erin said. "I'm just thinking. I can't control where my brain wants to go."

"Or your mouth," Lili said with a giggle, and Erin frowned.

"Hey!" Erin protested.

"Well, I can't stop thinking about it, either," Willow said. "The Rivals knew exactly where to look. It's almost like they heard our conversation with Principal Frederickson."

The girls were quiet for a moment, and then Jasmine's eyes got big.

"Maybe they did!" she said excitedly. "They could have planted a bug in Principal Frederickson's office."

Lili made a face. "Like a spider?"

"No, like a listening device," Jasmine said.

Willow nodded. "That's a good theory. Except that Principal Frederickson's office was alarmed, remember? But the alarm only went off when Aaron stole the diamond."

"And Principal Frederickson just started helping us anyway," Erin added. "So if they wanted to get information about the diamond, they probably would have bugged one of us."

Jasmine looked horrified. "Oh my gosh, what if they did?" she wondered. She lowered her voice to a whisper. "What if they're bugging us right now?"

"When would they have done that?" Willow asked. "We've only seem them a couple of times since the diamond was stolen in New York."

"Then maybe they did it in New York," Jasmine shot back. "Or maybe at one of the quiz bowl meets since then."

Erin suddenly clapped a hand over her mouth and pointed to Lili's Statue of Liberty pen. She slowly removed her hand. "What if they bugged one of our pens?" she whispered.

Jasmine, Willow, and Erin quickly dug in their backpacks and took out their pens. Then Erin began to unscrew the battery compartment.

"What are we looking for?" Lili asked.

"Something that doesn't belong," Erin whispered back.

Following Erin's lead, the other girls began to quietly unscrew the battery compartment on their own pens.

"I'm still not sure what we're looking for," Lili whispered.

After getting the compartment open, Erin slid the battery out from her pen. She held it up silently. It looked like a regular battery.

Willow did the same, as did Jasmine. Nothing looked unusual. But Lili's battery wasn't the only thing to fall out of her pen. A metal circle the size of a nickel landed in her palm, too.

"What's this?" Lili wondered, holding it up.

Erin grabbed the circle from her and quickly dropped it in Jasmine's water bottle.

"Hey!" Jasmine cried.

"Sorry," Erin said. "But I had to deactivate it. I saw it in a movie once. Now we can talk normally again."

Willow grabbed the bottle and held it up. "That sure looks like some kind of device. Lili, do you think Eli could tell us for sure?"

"Probably. I'll ask him," Lili said.

Jasmine sighed, took the bottle from Willow, and capped it. Then she handed it to Lili.

"It's all yours."

Lili looked at the device floating inside the bottle, and then suddenly got a panicked look on her face.

"Oh no! Does this mean the Rivals have been listening to *everything* I've been saying?" she asked.

"Only if you're near the pen," Erin answered.

Lili groaned. "This is awful! Sometimes I pretend that I'm a Japanese pop singer, and I've been using the pen as a microphone.

That means they've heard me sing the theme to the *Super Cute Happy Fun Hour*, like, a million times!"

Her friends tried to look mortified for Lili, but they couldn't hold it for long, and burst into giggles.

"I'm sorry, Lili, but that's too funny! I can just picture the Rivals sitting around, hoping to learn about diamonds, and instead hearing you sing songs from video games," Willow said.

Lili pouted, but slowly her frown turned into a smile. "I guess that *is* pretty funny."

"How come you never sing for us?" Erin teased. "We like super happy fun, too."

"No way!" Lili said, shaking her head and laughing.

Jasmine looked worried. "Lili, did you have the pen with you at the quiz bowl match on Saturday?"

Lili nodded. "I've been using it a lot. It's like my new lucky charm."

"But it shouldn't matter, because the Rivals already knew about the diamond then," Erin pointed out.

Willow and Jasmine looked at each other.

"But they didn't know about the emerald," Willow said.

"Exactly," Jasmine said, her eyes growing wide. "But now they do. They know that Derrica Girard has it."

"We've got to warn her!" Erin cried.

Chapter Nine

*J*asmine shook her head. "No way. Principal Frederickson told us to stay out of it."

Erin frowned. "Well, we should at least tell her that the Rivals know about the emerald."

"Then she'll think we're getting involved," Lili said. "I don't think I can face the Dragon Queen again today."

Willow looked thoughtful. "Maybe . . . maybe we could send Derrica a warning ourselves — tell her that someone is trying to steal the emerald. Then she could put it in a bank vault or something, and the Rivals would never get it."

Jasmine nervously rubbed the side of her nose. "That kind of sounds like getting involved to me."

Erin took out her cell phone and began to press buttons under the table. Cell phone use wasn't allowed during school hours.

"Let me check her Chatter feed," Erin said, ignoring Jasmine's objection. "Maybe we can contact her through there."

"You subscribe to her Chatter feed?" Willow asked in disbelief.

"I told you, Mary Ellen watches that dumb TV show," Erin said. "So I'm forced to watch it, too."

"And your sister forced you to follow Derrica's Chatter updates?" Jasmine asked with a grin.

Erin ignored her again. "Let's see. Right now she's filming the show."

"Well, *I* don't think it's a dumb show," Lili said. "They wear some amazing clothes."

"I kind of like all the drama," Jasmine admitted. "I mean, could you believe it when Lucille didn't invite Derrica to that party? They're supposed to be friends."

Willow shook her head. "Am I the only person in the world who doesn't watch *East Coast Class*?"

"Yes," answered her three friends at once.

"But didn't Principal Frederickson say it was hard to get in touch with Derrica?" Lili pointed out.

"Yeah," Erin said. "But we're cute sixth graders. We could say that we're working on a school project about her or something. People can't resist that. Flattery works on Derrica every time. If you've seen the show, you'll know. I could send her a message on Chatter."

"Don't!" Jasmine said quickly. "We've got to do this quietly, you know? Not so public."

Lili nodded. "Maybe we could write her a letter."

"I have a better idea," Willow said. "This TV show films in the DC area, right?"

The other girls nodded.

"Well, you need a permit to film anywhere, and those are public record," Willow said. "I know, because some movie filmed scenes at the community center once, and they needed my mom to sign forms and stuff."

"Oh, right. 'Cause she runs the place," Erin commented.

"Exactly," Willow said. "So what we need to do is find out where the show is going to be filming, and then show up in person."

"And then warn her that her necklace might be stolen?" Erin asked. "She might think we're weird."

Jasmine's green eyes sparkled with excitement. "I've got an idea. Maybe we could tell her that the necklace once belonged to Martha Washington, and ask her to donate it to the school."

"Why would she do that?" Willow asked skeptically.

"To look good on TV," Jasmine replied. "And once we get it, we can look for the next clue."

Willow frowned. "I'm not sure. I know it was my idea to approach her in person, but now I'm thinking it's too much."

Jasmine sighed. "There you go again. You only like your own ideas."

"I'm not saying that," Willow said defensively. "I'm just trying to think things through."

"Well, I think it's perfect," Erin interjected.

"We should do it," Lili urged.

Willow looked defeated. "Okay, then. I think I can look up the film permits online."

"I didn't realize you girls were such big fans of *East Coast Class*," said Lili's mom, Mrs. Higashida, as she drove down the tree-lined streets of River Park. Not far from Hallytown, the small village was known for its wealthy residents, high-end shops, and fancy restaurants.

"The show is really big in the sixth grade," Lili said, lying just a little bit.

"And you're sure the show is filming on Main Street?" she asked.

"The production company has a permit to film here all day," Willow explained.

Mrs. Higashida shook her head. "You girls are very resourceful. I don't think I would have gone through so much trouble to get an autograph when I was your age."

"It's the digital age, Mom," Lili said. "It's easy to find out this kind of stuff these days."

Her mother steered the car into a parking lot on a side street and found a space. "I've been meaning to check out the new shoe shop down here anyway. Promise me you'll stick together, and don't leave the street, okay?"

The girls promised, and then they headed back to Main Street with Lili's mom trailing behind them. In the center of the street, they saw a bunch of film equipment outside a restaurant.

"Ooh, that must be it!" Lili said excitedly.

The sign on the window read *Emile's Bistro*. They walked through the door into a long, rectangle-shaped space with warm orange walls and cozy wooden tables and chairs. All the way in the back of the room they could see bright lights and a man with a TV camera filming a table of glamorous-looking women.

Jasmine pointed to one with wavy blond hair who sat facing the doorway. A green gem glittered on a chain that hung around her neck.

"That's Derrica!" she exclaimed. "And she's wearing the emerald!"

Suddenly a man in a black suit appeared in front of them. His brown hair was slicked back and shiny.

"May I help you?" he asked, in a voice that clearly said he did not want to help them.

Erin spoke up. "We just want to talk to —"

"We're waiting for my parents," Willow interrupted her. "They're parking the car."

"Fine," the man said with a sniff. "Please move to the waiting area near the front of the restaurant. And be quiet. We're filming a very important show here."

"We'll be quiet as mice," Jasmine promised, flashing him a sweet smile, and the man walked back into the restaurant.

The girls took a seat in the foyer of the restaurant on a bench by the front door.

"So why the lie?" Erin asked Willow.

"If we said we wanted to talk to Derrica, he probably would have thrown us out," Willow explained. "This way, we have a reason to be here."

"But they'll make us leave when your parents don't show up, won't they?" Lili asked.

"We don't need that much time," Willow said. "We just need to talk to Derrica."

"How can we do that if they're filming?" Jasmine wondered.

Then they heard a loud voice from the back of the restaurant. "Take five, everybody! We need to reset the lights."

Willow grinned. "Perfect. I should probably go alone, so that manager guy doesn't notice."

"I'll go with you," Jasmine said quickly. "You need someone with you who knows the show."

"Fine," Willow said reluctantly. "Come on, let's move."

"Hey — what about us?" Erin asked. "I wouldn't mind meeting Derrica, too."

"We've got to keep this low-key," Willow insisted. "We can't all go barging back there or the manager will throw us out for sure. You and Lili can keep watch from the bench."

"Watch for what?" Erin asked.

Willow shrugged. "I don't know. But it can't hurt."

"I want a full report of what she is wearing," Lili called after them.

Willow and Jasmine quickly made their way to the back of the restaurant. Derrica was talking with a brunette wearing gaudy diamond earrings and a matching bracelet. Both women looked angry.

"That's Rhianna Alison," Jasmine whispered to Willow. "She and Derrica are always fighting."

As they got closer, they could hear what the women were saying.

"It's just not fair," Derrica complained. "I found Dion first. He's the only one who knows what to do with my hair!" She fluffed her wavy locks to make her point.

"It's a free country, Derrica," Rhianna shot back. "Dion's allowed to have more than one customer, you know."

Jasmine looked worried. "I'm not sure if we should interrupt them."

"It's now or never," Willow said. "Let's go."

But then a loud sound rang through the restaurant.

"Ca-caw! Ca-caw!"

"What is that?" Jasmine wondered.

At the front of the restaurant, they saw Erin with her hands cupped around her mouth.

"Oh no. What is she doing?" Willow asked.

Next to her, Lili was waving her arms and pointing to a nearby table. The girls looked over and saw two diners, each holding a menu in front of them. Then one of the customers lowered his menu — it was Ryan Atkinson!

He looked alarmed to see Willow and Jasmine there. Then he leaned forward and began to whisper to his companion, whom the girls realized was Isabel.

"We'd better hurry," Jasmine urged, and the two girls cautiously approached Derrica's table.

"Excuse me, Ms. Girard?" Willow asked. Her voice sounded nervous. Derrica turned, and at first she looked annoyed. But when she saw the two girls, she smiled.

"Yes, I'd be happy to give you an autograph," Derrica said brightly.

Thinking quickly, Jasmine rummaged through her bag and took

out a scrap of paper and a gel pen, which she handed to Derrica. Willow kept talking.

"Yes, that would be nice, but we've got something else to ask you about," Willow began. "It's about your emerald. You see —"

"Ahhhhhhhhhh!" Derrica shrieked, jumping out of her chair. Her green silk dress was soaked. It had all happened so quickly, but Willow soon put the pieces together — the spilled glass of water on the table, and Isabel Baudin hurriedly walking away, flashing a triumphant smile.

But Derrica didn't see Isabel. Her face red with fury, she turned to Rhianna.

"You are too much!" she yelled. "You're so jealous that you can't stand to see me get any attention from my fans!"

"Get over yourself!" Rhianna shouted back. "I can't help it if you're clumsy!"

A young man wearing a baseball cap ran up and tapped the cameraman. "Start filming! We've got to get this."

Willow pulled Jasmine away from the table. "We'd better get out of here," she hissed.

They raced to the front door, where they found the restaurant manager escorting Lili and Erin outside.

"Oh yeah? Well, I bet your food stinks anyway!" Erin was shouting.

Jasmine shrugged apologetically at the manager as she and Willow squeezed by.

"Sorry," she said.

Willow turned to Erin when they got outside.

"What was that?" she asked. *"Ca-caw?"*

"I was giving you a signal," Erin explained. "Lili spotted Ryan and Isabel at that table, and we wanted to warn you."

"You ended up warning *them* that we were there," Willow said, sounding exasperated.

Erin looked sheepish. "Sorry. I didn't think of that."

"They would have seen us anyway," Jasmine pointed out.

Willow sighed and leaned back against a tree. "Yeah, I know. It's just . . . we were so close!"

"At least I got her autograph," Jasmine said.

Lili looked excited. "Really? Cool!"

"Getting the emerald would have been better," Willow said gloomily.

"Well, look on the bright side," Jasmine said.

"What's that?" Willow asked.

Jasmine grinned. "That fight is going to make a great TV episode!"

Chapter Ten

"So the Rivals have beaten us again!" Jasmine said, flopping down on the fluffy rug on Lili's bedroom floor. Lili pushed a pile of clothes underneath her bed to make room for the rest of the girls.

"I wouldn't say that," Willow said. "After all, if the Rivals were planning on approaching Derrica, they didn't get a chance."

Erin grinned. "Willow, you really hate losing, don't you?"

"There's nothing to like about losing," Willow said flatly. "We need to regroup. The Rivals are clearly after Derrica and the necklace. If they get it, it's all over for us. They've already got the diamond and the ruby. We're not sure if they have the sapphire, too. So this could be our last chance. We have to beat them to it."

"When's the next time the show is filming?" Jasmine asked.

"I didn't see any more permits," Willow replied. "But they might be filming in someone's private house or something."

Lili jumped up and grabbed her laptop off her desk. She flipped it open and began to type.

"Maybe there's something on the show's blog," she suggested.

Erin opened her phone. "I'll check Derrica's Chatter page."

For a few minutes, the room was quiet except for the sound of tapping on keys.

"Derrica doesn't say anything about where she's going to be," Erin reported. "Mostly, she's just mad at Rhianna."

"Here's something," Lili piped up. "This says that the cast of *East Coast Class* is going to be at a big charity ball two weeks from tonight."

"I bet she'll wear the emerald there," Jasmine guessed.

"Probably," Erin said, still looking at the screen. "There's a quote here from her about the emerald. She calls it her 'lucky charm' and says she wears it everywhere!"

"Just like my lucky pen," Lili said.

Jasmine laughed. "Sure, if your pen was worth thousands of dollars."

Willow looked thoughtful. "So there's a good chance that the Rivals might try to get the emerald at the charity ball. But since Derrica wears it everywhere, they could strike at any time."

"We just need to tail Derrica," Erin said. "Like private investigators."

"Which would be great, except we go to school and don't drive and can't go out late at night," Jasmine pointed out.

"Tailing the Rivals would make more sense," Willow chimed in. "But that's not easy, either. It's too bad we don't have some way to keep tabs on them . . ."

A tall boy with spiky hair appeared in the doorway.

"I've been listening to you guys," said Lili's brother, Eli. "How come I'm not invited to this meeting? After everything I've done for you so far."

His voice was teasing, but all four Jewels immediately felt bad. Like they had told Principal Frederickson, Eli was an honorary Jewel, even if he did go to Atkinson Prep with the Rivals. Without Eli's help, the girls never would have been able to trick the Rivals into giving them the diamond that night in New York City.

"Come in, come in!" Jasmine and Erin said at once, scooting over to make room for him on the rug. Eli sat down, smiling.

"Thanks," he said. "Lili's been keeping me updated on the whole emerald thing. And she showed me that bug that was in her pen. Pretty sophisticated technology for a bunch of sixth graders."

"Well, they *do* have Arthur Atkinson helping them," Willow pointed out. "He's got tons of money and he must know where to get all kinds of sophisticated equipment."

"Equipment that helps people break into safes, for example," Erin piped up.

Eli nodded. "Yeah, that kind of stuff can get expensive. You might not be able to track the Rivals, but you could use a GPS device to keep track of their movements on a computer. But those will cost you a few hundred bucks."

Jasmine sat up straight, her eyes shining. "Wait, we have one of those!" she cried. "When we adopted Mozart from the pound, he used to run away all the time. He used to push open the gate and jump over the fence and everything. Mom and Dad finally got this little GPS thing to put in his collar so we could find him. Once he got used to being part of the family, he stopped, so we don't use it anymore."

"Awesome!" Erin said. "So we just need to put a collar around one of the Rivals and then we'll always know where they are!"

Eli laughed. "You wouldn't need a collar," he said. "You'd just have to hide it in something that one of the Rivals always has with them. Like they did with Lili's pen."

Lili frowned. "That was so unfair!"

"Exactly," Willow said. "I don't know if I feel right about this. It kind of feels like cheating."

"It's not cheating if we're doing the same thing," Erin countered.

"Yeah," agreed Jasmine. "We're just making things even."

Willow didn't answer right away. Instead, she absently poked at the purple strands of the rug.

"Come on, Willow," Erin said. "You hate losing, right? Well, we can't win without the right equipment. It's like playing basketball without a ball."

Erin's logic hit home, and Willow reluctantly relented. "Okay," she said. "But how do we do it, and who do we choose?"

"Ryan," Jasmine said firmly. "Anytime something important happens, he's usually there. He's the Rivals' team captain and he also seems to be leading their little gang of jewel thieves."

"And he's connected to Arthur," Erin pointed out. "Definitely Ryan."

Willow nodded. "Now we just have to hide the GPS on him somewhere."

All four Jewels stared at Eli.

"Oh, great," he said sarcastically. "Now I'm starting to wish I had never come in here. That's not going to be easy."

"But you go to the same school," Erin said.

"And you're sooooo good at this tech stuff," Jasmine added, buttering him up. "If anyone can do it, it's you."

"Plus, I'll let you have my dessert for a week," Lili added.

Eli held out his hand, and Lili shook it.

"Deal," he agreed, and he got a mock serious look on his face. "It's time to launch Operation Emerald!"

Chapter Eleven

Eli's heart pounded as the third-period bell rang. He quickly made his way down the hallways of Atkinson Prep. He had told his math teacher, Mr. Hardaway, that he was supposed to help Coach Peters with something, and he'd be late for class. It was a lie, but Eli knew that Mr. Hardaway and Coach Peters almost never talked. So Eli would probably be safe — if he hurried.

It felt weird to lie and sneak around, but exciting at the same time. And figuring out the plan hadn't been easy. First, he had to get the GPS from Jasmine and make sure it was working. On Monday and Tuesday, he'd watched Ryan as closely as he could without looking suspicious. Eli kept a careful list of everything Ryan wore and carried with him.

At first, placing it somewhere on Ryan's school uniform seemed like a good idea, until Eli realized that Ryan didn't wear the uniform out of school, when he'd be most likely to try to steal the emerald. Then Eli thought about putting the GPS in Ryan's shoes, but he might change those, too. Ryan's watch would have been perfect, because he almost never took it off. But the device was about an inch by an inch square — too big to effectively hide in a watch.

Finally, Eli figured it out. He didn't know why it took him so long to notice it, but after several days of reconnaissance, it became clear to Eli that Ryan was basically addicted to his new mini tablet device. He had the latest high-tech model, and he used it to go on Chatter, play games, and watch videos between classes. Tablets weren't allowed in school but none of the teachers stopped Ryan, because of his uncle. Nobody wanted to get chewed out by Arthur Atkinson.

Even better, Ryan had a thick, black protective case for his tablet, the kind that kept it from shattering if you dropped it. Eli went to the local tech store and examined a case just like Ryan's. If he could get the plastic open, there would be just enough room to slide in the GPS.

And now it was Friday, and Eli had just one chance to put Operation Emerald into action. Eli had noticed that the only time Ryan's tablet wasn't locked up was during gym class, when Ryan stuffed all of his belongings into an open cubbyhole in the locker room.

Eli stopped outside the locker room door and leaned against the wall. Inside, he could hear the boys talking and laughing loudly as they changed for gym. He nervously glanced up and down the hall. When the noise subsided, he slowly opened the door and peeked in.

Thankfully, the locker room was empty. He swiftly made his way to the cubbyholes. Though Eli had seen Ryan bring the tablet into the locker room with him throughout the week, he had never followed him in. Now he had to dig through the cubbyholes until he found it.

He struck gold in the sixth cubby he checked. He reached in his pocket for his tools and found that his palms were sweating. Planning the whole thing had been kind of exciting, but now that it was real, the pressure was pretty intense.

It's like Mission: Impossible *or something,* he thought, and then he forced himself to take a deep breath and calm down. He knew just what to do.

He used a small tool to pop open the case. Then he activated the GPS and slid it inside. But when he tried to close the case again, it wouldn't fit.

Eli started to sweat again. His measurements had been precise. It had to be stuck on something. Carefully, he tried to adjust the GPS using the slim tip of a screwdriver.

Then he heard a noise outside the door, from the gym entrance.

"Just one minute, Coach!"

Heart pounding, Eli pushed aside his panic and ran for the equipment bin and crouched down behind it, gripping the tablet tightly in his sweaty hands. Just a few feet away, he heard someone shuffling around in the cubbies. What if he got caught? It would look like he was trying to steal the tablet. His mother would freak out. Not to mention how embarrassing it would be to be thought of as a thief. And right now, he was the Jewels' last hope at stopping the Rivals. A lot was riding on this! Then he heard the sound of footsteps running away.

"Got it!" And then the gym door closed.

Eli realized he'd been holding his breath the whole time. He slowly got up and began to work on the tablet again, his hands shaking.

Focus! he told himself.

He fiddled with the case for another minute, and then he heard a satisfying snap. He'd done it!

Eli quickly replaced the tablet in Ryan's cubby, making sure he left everything just as he found it. It was done. Sure, there was a chance that Ryan might find the GPS, but what could he do? With any luck, he wouldn't find it, and the Jewels would have the upper hand.

Chapter Twelve

"Which of the following animals is a mollusk: an earthworm, a squid, or a turtle?"

Jasmine and Willow both hit the buzzer at the same time, but Willow's went off a split second earlier. The quiz bowl moderator nodded at her.

"Squid!" Willow replied confidently.

"Correct," said the moderator. "The Jewels are ahead by twenty points, so we do not need a bonus round. The Martha Washington Jewels win the match."

Erin and Lili grinned at each other. Willow tried to high-five Jasmine, but Jasmine's arms were firmly folded in front of her. Willow frowned and led the girls across the stage to shake hands with their opponents.

"Great job!" Ms. Keatley said as they left the stage. "You girls are on top of your game lately."

"Thanks!" replied Erin. Jasmine didn't even look at Ms. Keatley. She walked out into the hallway, and Willow followed her.

Ms. Keatley looked concerned. "Is everything okay?" she asked.

"We'll check it out," Erin said. She nodded to Lili, and the two girls went out into the hallway.

Jasmine and Willow were standing next to a water fountain, arguing.

"That was a science question," Jasmine was saying. "Those are supposed to be mine."

"We can't think like that!" Willow protested. "Our goal is to beat the other team. If any one of us knows the answer, we need to buzz in, no matter what the subject matter is."

Erin and Lili watched the argument from a distance.

"Did they always fight like this?" Lili asked. She'd just transferred to Martha Washington at the start of sixth grade, so Lili had only known the girls for a few months. But Willow, Jasmine, and Erin had been together since kindergarten.

"Once in a while," Erin replied. "They've always been best friends, you know? I used to feel left out sometimes until you came along."

Lili's face melted. "Oh, that's so sweet!"

"Anyway, I think it's the stress of this whole Rivals thing that's setting them off this time," Erin explained. "Honestly, this drama is getting to me. It's worse than a reality show!"

Lili giggled. "That would be a great show. *The Real Contestants of Quiz Bowl.*"

Erin laughed. "Right. An inside look at the super-glamorous world of quiz bowl." Then her eyes lit up. "Wait a second! You have video on your cell, right?"

Lili held up her pink, sparkly phone. "Yup! Why?"

"Start filming," Erin told her.

Lili pressed a button and followed Erin as she headed down the hall toward Jasmine and Willow.

"But what if you didn't know the answer?" Willow was saying.

"But I did!" Jasmine said loudly. "It's like you want to be the whole team by yourself!"

Erin started circling the girls, talking. "On this week's episode of *The Real Contestants of Quiz Bowl*, sparks fly as Jasmine and Willow duke it out by the water fountain," she narrated.

Jasmine and Willow ignored her and kept on fighting.

"And what about when you didn't give me credit for the theory I had when we were talking to Principal Frederickson? The one about the Rivals stealing the diamond before quiz bowl and doing something else to trigger the alarm while they were onstage. You made it sound like it was everyone's idea, not mine!" Jasmine said angrily.

"Whoa!" Willow held her hands up in surprise. "Seriously? Do you honestly think I'd deliberately not give you credit for an idea you had? A lot was going on when we found out the diamond had been stolen. And your theory was wrong, so I don't know why you're so eager to get recognition for it."

Jasmine stomped her feet in anger. "See what I mean? You can be so . . . so . . . frustrating! Whether it's quiz bowl, or basketball, or stopping the Rivals, you act like you're the one who is in charge."

Erin, desperate to get the girls to stop fighting, continued with her "reality show" narration. "Things get hot onstage when the questions are flying, but they're even hotter in the hallway!"

Lili joined in. "And once again, the contestants' outfits are totally fashion forward," she said. "Both Jasmine and Willow are rocking their red team T-shirts. Jasmine is accenting hers with black leggings and ballet flats, while Willow is going for a sporty look with skinny jeans and white sneakers. Fabulous!"

Jasmine and Willow finally noticed what was going on around them. They stopped and looked at Erin and Lili.

"You two are crazy," Willow said.

"Yeah, crazy about tacos," Erin said. "Come on. The moms are taking us for lunch at Veggie Juan's, and then we're going to Lili's."

"I don't know," Jasmine said. She still looked upset.

"Come on, Jazz. Eli and I set up a bunch of stuff last night," Lili said. "I can't wait to show you."

Jasmine reluctantly agreed, but she wouldn't even look at Willow.

During a lunch of vegetable tacos piled with beans, lettuce, tomatoes, peppers, mushrooms, zucchini, and cheese, Jasmine and Willow barely spoke — but at least they had stopped fighting. After lunch, Mrs. Higashida brought them all back to Lili's house. The girls paused in the foyer to remove their shoes and were surprised to see a bunch of shoes already neatly lined up against the wall.

"What's going on?" Lili asked.

"It's Obaasan," replied her mother. "Your grandmother is doing her dance exercise class here."

Lili peeked into the living room and smiled, then led the Jewels upstairs.

"There you are," Eli said, standing in the doorway of his room. "Come on in."

Spare and clean, Eli's room was the opposite of Lili's. His white walls had no posters on them, and his bed was neatly made with a black bedspread. One wall of his room was taken up with a long computer desk and tons of gadgets and wires neatly stored in stacked and labeled metal bins. The only thing that looked out of place was a big, colorful poster on an easel with a photo of Derrica Girard in the middle.

"What's all this?" Jasmine asked.

"First, let me show you the GPS," he said, sliding into his computer chair. He started typing. "See? I just need to send a signal to the GPS, and then it tells me where it is."

"Wow. We really could have used a tracker on the Rivals back in New York City," Jasmine said, looking at the gadgets neatly laid out on Eli's desk.

"The Rivals didn't compete in the match this morning," Willow explained. "I was worried that they were out stealing Derrica's emerald."

"I don't think so," Eli said. "Ryan's been home all morning. And Derrica's been at a beauty salon."

"How did you know that? We don't have a GPS on her," Erin pointed out.

Lili walked to the poster and smiled proudly. "We don't need one. She's constantly updating her Chatter status. And she posts tons of stuff about herself on her blog. It's like she doesn't care about privacy at all."

"I guess not, if she's on a reality TV show," Jasmine mused.

"So, anyway, I worked on this all last night," Lili said. She pointed to a box on the chart. "Over here is a rough weekly schedule that Eli and I came up with after going back and tracking her posts for the last month. And this box is all her favorite shops, and that one shows her favorite restaurants."

The girls stepped up to the board to get a closer look.

"Awesome," Erin said admiringly. "You would make a great stalker."

"That's not all," Lili said. She walked to Eli's desk and picked up a green folder. She took out a photo of Derrica wearing a red dress and handed it to Willow.

"What's this?" Willow asked.

"She posted the dress she's wearing to the charity ball next week," Lili explained. "And see around her neck? She's not going to wear the emerald because it clashes with the red. Instead, a famous jewelry guy is going to lend her a ruby and diamond necklace."

"Wow!" Jasmine said. "That's going to be gorgeous."

Willow looked thoughtful. "So she won't have the emerald with her on Saturday, which means the Rivals won't be trying to steal it."

"Not exactly," Eli said, spinning around in his chair to face them. "She's going to be staying at the hotel that night, so the necklace might be in her room."

Erin nodded. "I remember that quote we found. 'It's my lucky charm. I take it with me everywhere.'"

"And if it's in the room . . ." Lili began.

". . . it will be even easier for the Rivals to steal," Willow finished. "A lot easier than stealing it off someone's neck in the middle of a big party."

"We've got to find a way to get to that charity ball!" Erin exclaimed.

"Maybe not," Jasmine said. "Lili and Eli found out a lot about Derrica's schedule. If we can get to her before the ball, we won't have to worry about it."

"Well, we don't know every move she makes," Lili admitted. "But we have a pretty good idea. That's how we figured out she would be at the beauty parlor this morning. But after that, it's just a guess."

"Well, we could try," Jasmine said. "Maybe figure out the most likely places she'll be, and try to go there."

"It's worth a try," Willow said, and Jasmine caught her eyes.

"Thanks," Jasmine said.

"Hold on!" Eli cried suddenly. "Ryan's been moving."

"Where to?" Erin asked, looking over his shoulder.

"He's in River Park," Eli said. "Let's see where he goes. He's still on the move. Looks like he's headed toward Tinker Street."

Lili ran back to the easel. "Elan's Couture is on that street! It's one of Derrica's favorite clothing shops."

"Do you think she's there, and Ryan knows it?" Jasmine wondered.

"Can you check that thing from your phone?" Willow asked Eli.

Eli nodded. "Yeah. Why?"

"Because if Ryan's on the move, we need to be, too," she said. "Maybe he's also tracking Derrica, and she's at the shop right now!"

"But how are we going to get to River Park?" Jasmine wondered.

Lili grinned and hurried to the doorway.

"Mom!"

Chapter Thirteen

"Mom said she'd drive us. Eli, are you coming?" Lili asked.

"I'm not sure I'd know what to do at a fancy women's clothing store with you guys. I'll stay here and keep you posted by text of Ryan's movements, so keep your phone handy," Eli said.

Mrs. Higashida agreed to give the girls a ride, although she seemed confused. "The shops on Tinker Street are very expensive," she remarked. "Way out of the budget of your allowances, I'm sure."

"You know me, Mom," Lili replied. "I'll study the latest fashions and make my own versions." It was the truth. While they were tracking down Ryan, Lili couldn't help but be excited to check out the designs at Elan's Couture.

"Lili's are always better, anyway," Erin said proudly. Even though Erin got dressed most days by throwing on the nearest T-shirt and jeans, she admired Lili's unique sense of style.

Mrs. Higashida stopped at the gate of the parking lot on Tinker Street and grabbed a ticket. "Even parking is expensive here," she complained as she parked the car.

"Mom, you're the best!" Lili said. "I'll pay you back with a custom design after I get some inspiration today, I promise."

Mrs. Higashida smiled at her daughter. "Don't worry about it, sweetie. While you girls are window-shopping I am going to stop by that new gourmet olive oil and vinegar store. Everyone at work has been raving about it, so this gives me the perfect opportunity to check it out."

As they walked out onto Tinker Street, Mrs. Higashida reminded the girls to stay on the street and stick together. She turned right while the girls headed left, toward Elan's Couture.

Tinker Street was located in the historic section of River Park. The girls walked down the cobblestone sidewalk, admiring the pretty old brick buildings. Jasmine shivered as they passed a clothing boutique, and it wasn't from the crisp breeze that was blowing.

"That business suit looks like something Principal Frederickson would wear," Jasmine said nervously as she pointed at a shop window. "What if we bump into her here? And she finds out we're still trying to stop the Rivals?"

Lili grabbed Jasmine's hand and gave it a little squeeze. "Relax," she said. "The odds of that are, like, a billion to one."

"Not really," Willow said. "Mathematically speaking, depending on where Principal Frederickson shops, the odds could be much higher, especially considering this is a Saturday and the busiest shopping day of the week."

Lili groaned. "Not helpful!"

Willow shrugged. "Maybe not, but it's realistic."

"So what if she is shopping on Tinker Street?" Erin asked. "We don't have to tell her what we're doing here, and there is no reason why we wouldn't be shopping here, too."

Jasmine pointed to a pair of gold and diamond hoop earrings in the next shop's window. "There's one reason. Those earrings cost three thousand dollars!"

"Hey, maybe we won the lottery." Lili laughed. "That would explain it."

"Puh-leeze!" Erin said dramatically. "Even if we won the lottery my mother still wouldn't let me spend that kind of money. Unless I did a bazillion chores around the house to earn it. And, Willow, that *is* mathematically correct, trust me!"

Willow smiled. "I understand that math. My mom would be the same way!"

Lili's phone gave a beep. "It looks like Ryan *is* in Elan's Couture. Eli just texted me."

"We better hurry," Willow said as she quickened her pace. The other girls hurried after her.

After walking about a block, they arrived at the boutique. Willow stopped short in front of the door. "Um, guys?" she asked. "I don't think we thought this out. Do we all just go barreling in? We don't want to let on to Ryan that we're tracking his movements."

"If he sees us, I really don't think his first thought will be that we planted a GPS on him," Jasmine said curtly.

Willow's eyes flashed. "Maybe not, but don't you think it would be better to hang back and see what he's doing? If he knows we're watching him, he won't do something to give his plan away."

"I'll go in first and check out the layout," Lili suggested. "Don't worry, I'll keep it on the down low."

Lili stepped slowly through the door. A little bell chimed, signifying her presence to the salesclerks. A woman with a sleek blond bob, wearing a black dress and high heels, smiled at her.

"Good afternoon," she said to Lili. "Let me know if I can assist you with anything."

Lili nodded as her eyes traveled around the store. The walls were painted a deep pink. The black ceiling had recessed lighting with a black and silver chandelier hanging from the middle. A zebra-print couch and black-and-white polka-dotted chairs were scattered around the room. Small tables held clothing and accessories on them, as did the shelves lining the walls. More clothes hung from bars on some of the shelves. It was a combination of elegant, funky, and fun — and had the feel of shopping in a hip friend's house rather than at a store.

Oh wow, Lili thought. *They even have a designer vintage section.* She smacked her palm to her forehead. *Focus! You're not here to shop.*

There were a couple of other people shopping in this section. Both were women, and Ryan was nowhere in sight. Openings on the left and right of the room led to other spaces in the shop.

Lili smiled at the saleswoman as she turned to leave. "I'm just going to get my friends," she explained. "I'll be back."

Lili rushed outside and explained the layout of the store. "So, it looks like there are at least three different sections," she said. "Maybe more. I didn't see Ryan, but he must be in there somewhere."

Willow nodded. "Okay," she said. "We should split up."

Jasmine frowned. "I think we should stick together."

Erin shot Lili a look that clearly said "here we go again" before jumping in.

"How about you and Willow stick together in the main room," Erin suggested, "and I'll take the room on the left, and Lili can take the room on the right?"

Willow and Jasmine both nodded. "But we've got to be as low-key as possible," Willow said. "We shouldn't draw any attention to ourselves. Keep your cell phones handy. If anyone spots either Ryan or Derrica, text the others."

The girls agreed to the plan and headed into the store. The same saleswoman greeted them. Erin headed to the room on the left, Lili took off toward the right, and Willow and Jasmine browsed in the center room.

Lili's eyes grew wide as she entered the section that housed the couture, one-of-a-kind gowns. This room was done in deep gold tones, with glittery accents. Mannequins that looked like marble statues dotted the room, each one wearing a dress more fabulous than the last.

She reached a hand up to gently touch the flowing teal strapless gown on the mannequin closest to her. It was gorgeous!

"Elan! I love it!" a loud voice interrupted her. She ducked behind the mannequin and peeked around. It was Derrica! She was coming out of a dressing room, wearing a strapless cream-colored gown with a silver beading swirl detail. *It's stunning*, Lili thought in awe. Lili checked to see if she was wearing the emerald, but Derrica wasn't. A slim man with dark hair and skin, wearing a vibrant plaid suit with cowboy boots, fussed over her.

"You are my muse! I think of you and the heavens open and deposit the most beautiful ideas right here." He tapped the temple of his head with a finger. He had a slight accent, but Lili couldn't place it.

"You're too sweet. I'll take it!" Derrica said. "It will be perfect for that movie premiere I'm going to next month."

"I'll have to make a few adjustments to get it just right," Elan said. "While you are here, we can do a final fitting on the red gown, yes? I want it to fit you like a glove for the ball."

"Oh, darling, I wish I could but I've got to run." Derrica sighed. "I'm filming this afternoon. Supposedly Rhianna wants to apologize over lunch," she sniffed. "As if."

Derrica ducked back into the dressing room while Elan hovered outside. "I'll be in touch. We'll do it early next week," she called to him through the door.

Lili grabbed her phone to start texting the others about Derrica being in the store.

Willow read the text. "Lili says she'll be leaving soon. Now's our chance to try and warn her."

Derrica breezed so quickly out of the couture room that Lili didn't get a chance to talk to her. But when she walked into the main room, Jasmine and Willow were waiting.

"Excuse me," Jasmine started to say, but Willow stepped in front of her. "Ms. Girard, could I talk to you?" Willow asked.

Derrica stopped and smiled at her. "Hi!" she said. "Hey, I recognize you. You're the girls who asked for my autograph at Emile's Bistro. Right before Rhianna dumped a glass of water on me." She rolled her eyes, then laughed. "She'll do anything for camera time! Are you shopping here, too? Don't you just love it?"

Jasmine nodded. "It's a great store, but we wanted to talk to you about something —"

Just then, Derrica's cell phone began to ring. "Sorry," she said. "I've got to take this."

"Hi," she said. "Yes, I'm on my way. How could I be late? She said lunch was at two. Well, it's not my fault if she changed it at the last minute without telling me." She saw the girls waiting. "Hold on a sec," she said into the phone. "So, you wanted to tell me something?"

Willow nodded. "Yes, it's about your emerald necklace —"

"Oh, yes, it's my favorite!" Derrica said. "And I know exactly what you're going to say."

Willow and Jasmine exchanged worried glances. How could Derrica know the Rivals were trying to steal her necklace?

"You want me to start my own jewelry line and make copies of it to sell!" Derrica said triumphantly. "It's the number-one request my fans have. And I'll let you in on a secret." She lowered her voice.

"I'm in talks with several home-shopping networks about selling my new jewelry line. You know what, you girls are so cute, write down your addresses for me and I'll have my assistant send you each a necklace as soon as they roll off the production line." Derrica beamed at them.

"That's so nice," Jasmine gushed. "But we're worried someone is trying to steal your necklace. The real one. Now."

Derrica laughed. "Aren't you adorable? Don't worry your pretty heads about that. My necklace is totally fine. In fact, it's locked up in my hotel room safe as we speak. No one can get it!"

"But, Derrica —" Willow pleaded.

"Sorry, girls, but I've got to run!" she said as she sailed out the door. "I'm late!"

Jasmine whirled angrily toward Willow. "Why did you step in front of me when I was trying to talk to Derrica?"

"It was really important. I thought I should handle it," Willow said.

"Why? Because no one else but you can do things right?" Jasmine fumed. "Well, guess what? You failed. Derrica didn't believe us."

"Maybe if you had let me do all the talking, I could have convinced her," Willow said, annoyed. "But you had to butt in."

Jasmine's eyes flashed furiously. "Butt in? Excuse me. Nobody can get in the way of Queen Willow, right?"

"Not if you're going to mess things up!" Willow shot back.

That was the last straw for Jasmine. She shook her head, her curls whipping around her face.

"You think you can do everything yourself? Fine!" she said angrily. "I quit!"

"What do you mean, you quit?" Willow asked in disbelief.

"Everything," Jasmine said firmly. "Jewels. Saving the emerald. Being your friend. I'm done!"

Willow watched, stunned, as Jasmine took her phone out of her pocket and pressed a button. "Mom? Can you pick me up? I want to come home now."

Jasmine walked out of the store to wait for her mother. Willow started to go after her, but her phone beeped. It was Erin, letting her know that Ryan was indeed in the store!

Erin had entered the room that held shoes, jewelry, and some more dresses. As soon as she walked in, she spotted Ryan standing by a long glass display case at the end of the room. Luckily his back was to her. She ducked behind a rack full of dresses to spy on him.

"How can I help you today, Ryan?" a saleswoman asked him.

"My mother's birthday is coming up," Ryan said smoothly. "I know this is her favorite store and I was hoping you might have some suggestions about what she would like."

"Of course," the saleswoman answered. "She's lucky to have such a kind and thoughtful son."

Erin repressed a snort. *Yeah, right, he's a regular saint*, she thought.

The woman began removing some jewelry from the display case. "I know she was admiring these the last time she was in," she said to Ryan as she held up a pair of earrings.

"I remember her talking about a bracelet," Ryan said. "Something with her birthstone?"

"Oh, yes." The woman nodded. "The diamond bracelet. It's set in white gold." She removed it from the case and handed it to Ryan for his inspection.

"It's perfect," he said. "I'll take it."

The saleswoman rang up the bracelet and named a price that made Erin's jaw drop. Ryan simply handed over a credit card.

"Would you like the bracelet gift-wrapped?" the woman asked.

As Erin intently eavesdropped, she didn't notice the saleswoman who walked up behind her.

"Ahem!" the woman cleared her throat. Erin jumped.

"Can I help you with something?" she said curtly, taking in Erin's jeans, untied sneakers, and hoodie. Erin instantly panicked.

"Yes! I want to try this on!" She grabbed the nearest dress.

The saleswoman looked at her and raised an eyebrow. "You want to try on a wedding dress?"

Erin took a closer look at the rack of dresses she had been hiding behind. They were all in different shades of white — and they were all wedding dresses! She tried to think fast.

"I'm playing the Snow Queen in our school play," Erin said, saying the first thing that came into her mind.

"Our wedding dresses start at fifteen thousand dollars," the woman said haughtily.

"You should see our plays." Erin kept her excuse going, even though it was totally lame. She didn't know what else to do! "They are off the charts. The costumes are amazing. We even do a red carpet before the show."

"Mmmm-hmmmm," the saleswoman said while twisting her mouth into a scowl. She wasn't buying it.

Erin craned her neck around the woman to see Ryan turning to leave. She ducked farther back behind the rack of dresses and pointed at one.

"How about this one?" she whispered loudly. "How much does this cost?"

The saleswoman sighed. "That one is twenty-five thousand dollars.

Times certainly have changed. When I was in school plays, my mother made my costume."

"My mom making the costume! Gee, why didn't I think of that?" Erin asked. "Great idea! Thanks." She grabbed the woman's hand and shook it as she watched Ryan leave the room. He hadn't spotted her.

The saleswoman was looking at Erin like she had two heads. She withdrew her hand from Erin's disdainfully.

"I guess I'll be going now. Yep, got to get started on that angel costume, I mean Snow Queen costume," Erin said as she backed out of the door. The saleswoman crossed her arms and watched her leave.

Erin raced out into the main room. Willow had just watched Ryan leave the store. He hadn't spotted her, either.

"Let's get out of here!" Erin hissed. The saleswoman followed Erin out, watching her with a frown.

Lili came out of the couture gown room with a dreamy look in her eyes.

"Wow, those dresses are amazing," she told her friends. "Hey, where's Jasmine?"

Willow sighed. "I've got something to tell you."

"Fine," Erin said. "But it's time to leave. Tell us outside. I've shopped until she," Erin nodded at the saleswoman, "wants to drop me!"

Chapter Fourteen

"It's so weird studying for quiz bowl without Jasmine," Lili said sadly.

"Yeah, it makes it hard to concentrate," Erin echoed Lili's thought. "It's not the same."

"Jasmine is the one who decided to quit," Willow said defensively. "I didn't tell her to do that. She just went crazy! You know her. She's such a drama queen."

"We've all been under a lot of stress," Lili said soothingly. "Between school, quiz bowl, and knowing that this might be our last chance to stop the Rivals — it's enough to make anyone lose it."

Erin sighed as she flopped on Willow's bed. "It still stinks! We don't have an alternate for our team. If Jasmine doesn't compete with us, it's the end of the Jewels."

"She'll be back," Willow said confidently. "Once she cools down."

It was the next day and Erin and Lili were at Willow's house, trying to get in some quiz bowl study time.

"Ahem!" Willow said loudly. "Sneakers!"

"What?" Erin looked puzzled. Then she glanced at her feet on Willow's bed. "Oh, right, sorry," she said, and removed them.

"Your room sure is clean." Lili looked around admiringly. Willow's bed was perfectly made, her desk and nightstand uncluttered. Nothing was out of place or lying on the floor. "My mother would love it if I kept my room like this. I can't even shut my closet doors because of all the stuff I have crammed inside."

"It's hard for me to concentrate when things are messy," Willow admitted.

Erin laughed. "It's been so long since I've seen the floor of my room, I've forgotten what color the carpet is! But seriously, Willow, have you tried to talk to Jasmine?"

Willow shook her head. "I don't know what to say. I don't think I did anything wrong.

"You really believe it was okay to cut Jasmine off in order to talk to Derrica?" Lili asked gently. "If Jasmine had done that to you, how would you feel?"

Willow sighed. "You're right. I think Jasmine is super-smart. I always have. I can't explain it. I just get this feeling sometimes that I need to do things myself or else they won't get done right."

"Typical type-A personality." Erin nodded knowingly. "My sister Mary Ellen is exactly like that, too."

"Gee, thanks, I know how much you *love* Mary Ellen," Willow said sarcastically.

Erin laughed. "She's okay. She has her good points, too — and so do you and Jasmine. We need to be a team again."

Willow nodded. "You're right. I'll call her after we're done here."

They returned to studying, taking turns asking questions from the quiz bowl study cards Ms. Keatley had given them, but the conversation drifted back to yesterday's events.

"Do you think it was only a coincidence that Ryan and Derrica were at Elan's Couture at the same time?" Willow wondered.

"There are no coincidences where the Rivals are concerned," Erin said with conviction. "Trust me on that. Too bad for Ryan that Derrica wasn't wearing the emerald."

"Too bad for us that Derrica wouldn't take us seriously," Willow said.

Erin sighed. "I guess there are disadvantages to being 'cute' sixth graders, after all," she said, quoting Derrica's own words.

"It makes me more certain than ever that the Rivals are going to try and steal the emerald the night of the charity ball," Willow said decisively. "They've already proven once that they know how to crack a safe. But how can we be there to stop them?"

They were all silent as they thought about it.

"Teleportation?" Erin joked, but no one laughed.

"How did Ryan know Derrica was going to be at the boutique?" Willow wondered. "Derrica didn't mention it on Chatter until after she had left."

"Derrica shops there a lot," Lili reminded her. "It's her favorite store. It probably was just a lucky guess."

"He seemed to know the salespeople there," Erin replied. "At least one of them knew him by name. He probably buys all his mom's gifts there. Maybe he asked one of them to call him if Derrica came."

Willow nodded. "Stores like that will do anything to make their customers happy. Especially if they spend a lot of money."

Erin snorted. "No problem there. He's got an unlimited expense account thanks to his family's credit card. It must be nice to come from a rich family like that."

Lili sighed. "How are we ever supposed to beat the Rivals? They've got help and money that we don't."

Willow got a determined look in her eyes. "We beat them before and we can do it again!"

"All this studying has made me hungry," Erin said. "What do you say, time for a snack break, Willow?"

They trooped down to Willow's kitchen, a cozy, country-style room with wooden floors, ceiling beams, and white cabinets. It had sliding glass doors that overlooked the backyard. Outside they could see Willow's father tossing a football with her brothers Michael and Alex. Mrs. Albern sat at the kitchen table, feeding two-year-old Jason lunch in his high chair.

"Awwwww," Lili cooed. She went over to the high chair and leaned over Jason to say hi.

"Watch out!" Mrs. Albern tried to warn her, but it was too late. Jason flicked his little toddler spoon at Lili, spraying her with pasta.

"Jason!" Mrs. Albern scolded. Jason looked at Lili with a grin that could melt anyone's heart. "I sowwy," he said with a cute lisp.

Willow ruffled his hair as Mrs. Albern explained. "He's going through a phase right now of flinging his food at everyone. That's why I'm feeding him while his brothers are outside. And that's also why he's not allowed to have red sauce with his pasta."

Jason smiled up at his big sister. "He gets away with everything," Willow said as she smiled back at him. "He's just too cute."

"I cute!" Jason said as he continued to eat.

They all laughed as Willow took some apples out of the refrigerator and Lili cleaned herself off with some paper towels. Willow started to slice the fruit. "Are apples and peanut butter okay?"

"Yum! Sounds good to me," Erin said.

The girls took seats at the kitchen table as Willow got their snack ready.

"Have you ever been to Elan's Couture, Mrs. Albern?" Lili asked. "We were there yesterday, and the dresses are so gorgeous!"

Mrs. Albern smiled. "Believe it or not, Elan and I go way back," she said. "Our mothers were friends when we were growing up. I knew him before he had his fake European accent! He's a good guy. He just puts on a show for his customers."

Lili grew excited. "Maybe you could introduce me to him. I'd love to learn his fashion secrets."

"The next time his mom stops by the community center, I'll mention it to her," Mrs. Albern said. As manager of the Hallytown Community Center, she seemed to know everybody in town. Suddenly, Mrs. Albern frowned. "All this talk of couture reminds me — I need to figure out what I'm wearing for the charity ball! I have a few dresses in mind, but I'm not sure. And time is running out."

Willow looked at her mother in surprise as she placed the plate of apple slices and a bowl of peanut butter on the table. "You're going to the charity ball? How come you didn't tell me?"

Mrs. Albern smiled. "It slipped my mind. I've been so busy with work and the boys, I really haven't had time to think about it."

"Did you know that real-life celebrities like Derrica Girard will be there?" Lili asked. "It's going to be a huge event."

"Yeah, how did you get invited?" Erin asked. Everyone stopped munching and looked at her. "Uh, I didn't mean you're not important enough, Mrs. Albern. You know I think you're the greatest!"

Mrs. Albern laughed. "That's okay, Erin. No offense taken. I was invited because of the work I do at the community center, mostly for the volunteer programs I help organize. To tell you the truth, I'm not super-excited about going. It's a lot of work to get all dressed up. It's easy for your dad. He just has to rent a tux."

"You are so lucky!" Lili said. "If I could, I would go in your place."

"Me, too!" Erin nodded.

Mrs. Albern's face brightened. "I have an idea. The community center was asked to provide volunteers for the coat check at the event. I know it's not the same as being a guest, but you'll get to see everyone who comes in and check out what they're wearing. Even the celebrities like me." She chuckled.

Willow exchanged glances with Lili and Erin. They couldn't believe how lucky they were!

"Wow! Really?" Lili asked. "That would be awesome."

"Count me in!" Erin said.

Willow agreed, "And me!"

"Then it's settled," Mrs. Albern said. "I'll talk to your parents about it, girls. Do you think Jasmine would be interested in going, too? I know she couldn't make practice today, but I could ask her mother."

"I'll ask her and let you know," Willow said quickly. She hadn't told her mother about the fight with Jasmine.

Mrs. Albern nodded. "Let me know. Mr. Albern and I can take you with us. Although I wish it was settled about what I'm going to wear."

Lili stood up and gave Mrs. Albern a big hug. "Thanks so much! And don't worry about what you're going to wear. I'll totally help you. It's, like, my favorite thing to do."

Mrs. Albern returned Lili's hug. "Thanks! Why not? Just don't dress me like a teenybopper, okay?"

"Of course not!" Lili said. "I'm thinking dramatic elegance."

Mrs. Albern laughed. "Elegance is okay, but I'm not sure about the dramatic part."

"Can I look through your closet?" Lili asked eagerly.

"When I put Jason down for his nap, we can look together." Mrs. Albern sounded amused.

The girls finished their snack and raced up the stairs. They couldn't wait to talk in private about their lucky break. They rushed into Willow's room and she shut the door behind them.

"At least we'll be on the scene," Willow said with a smile on her face. "If the Rivals try to steal the emerald from Derrica's hotel room during the charity ball, we'll be nearby." But her smile slowly turned to a frown. "I wish Jasmine was here for this news. She'd be so excited."

"Call her already!" Erin yelled.

Willow picked up her phone and hit the button for Jasmine's number, but she didn't pick up. Willow left a message instead. "Hi, Jasmine. I'm really sorry about what happened yesterday. We need to talk. And I've got some exciting news. We'll be working the coat check for the charity ball. I hope you'll join us. We don't feel like a team without you. Call me back, okay? Bye."

"Awwwww," Lili said.

"I hope she comes back," Erin said. "This could be our last chance to stop the Rivals. They think they are so smart, but they are no match for us. No match for ALL of us, that is. We need to be a complete team again to win."

The girls exchanged nervous glances. Would they be able to defeat the Rivals without Jasmine?

Chapter Fifteen

The school week leading up to the ball was a busy time, filled with tests and quiz bowl practices. But Jasmine didn't return Willow's phone calls or texts, and she spoke only briefly with Erin and Lili during lunch. It was clear she was still hurting.

Even Ms. Keatley tried talking with her.

"It seems Jasmine is still very upset," she reported to Erin, Lili, and Willow afterward. "I'm afraid we'll have to find a new Jewels member, or we're going to have to forfeit our next match."

"No!" Willow said quickly. "We'll convince her to come back, Ms. Keatley. We promise."

Erin looked skeptical. "And if we can't, we'll forfeit. It's just not the Jewels without Jasmine."

While they waited for Jasmine to change her mind, the Jewels had no choice but to carry on their plans without her. They kept tabs on Derrica as best as they could and Eli texted during the week to let them know Ryan's movements, which were pretty boring and normal.

It made the girls believe more than ever they were right about the Rivals planning to steal the emerald the night of the charity ball. But would they be able to put a stop to whatever the Rivals had planned?

"We'll just have to be ready for anything," Willow said to Erin as they sat in Willow's living room the night of the ball, waiting. They wore white button-down shirts and black pants for their coat-check uniforms. Lili was upstairs, helping Mrs. Albern get ready.

Willow looked uncharacteristically stressed. Erin decided to make a joke to break the tension. She leapt to her feet and pretended to interview herself, holding up a hand to her mouth like it was a microphone.

"I'm here with Erin Fischer, live from the red carpet. Tell me, Erin, who are you wearing tonight? You look fabulous," she said in a fake newscaster voice.

She stepped to the side and beamed like a movie star. "Why, thank you. This shirt is an exclusive, one-of-a-kind hand-me-down from Mary Ellen Fischer. You can hardly see the mustard stain on the sleeve." She held up her sleeve with a flourish. "And the pants are from my marching band uniform. Note the stylish, shiny, light black stripes down the side." She pointed to the side of her leg.

It worked. Willow cracked up, holding on to her sides while she rolled around on the couch with laughter.

"What's so funny?" Mrs. Albern asked as she walked into the room, Lili at her side.

Willow sat up straight. "Wow, Mom, you look gorgeous!"

Mrs. Albern was wearing a black, sleeveless, knee-length lace dress with a V-neck. Her hair was styled into soft, cascading curls around her face.

Lili glowed. "Don't you love this dress? It looks just like a Dolce and Gabbana frock from their spring collection. I almost fainted when I saw this in her closet!"

Mrs. Albern laughed. "Trust me, it's not an actual designer dress, but I do like it, especially with Lili's styling."

She wore peep-toe high heels with bow accents and held a black beaded clutch. Around her wrist dangled a sapphire and rhinestone bracelet, which matched the earrings and necklace she wore, giving a pop of color to the outfit.

"Don't forget your wrap!" Lili said, handing over the evening scarf she was holding. It was sapphire blue with sequins scattered across it. Mrs. Albern put it over her shoulders and the look was complete.

"Lili, you should do this for a living!" Erin exclaimed.

Lili blushed. "Thanks. It's just fun for me," she said modestly. She, too, wore a white button-down shirt and black pants, although Lili added a splash of color with some funky pink and teal extensions woven into her black hair.

They piled into Mr. Albern's SUV while Willow's brothers waved from the front door with their aunt Denise, who was babysitting them for the night. Mr. Albern looked stylish in his black tuxedo. "We are one snazzy couple," he said to his wife as he held open the car door for her.

The Hotel River Park was located a block up from Tinker Street, also in the historic part of town. The entire street was lit with white lights in the trees, making it look very picturesque. Mr. Albern pulled ahead of the news vans that were parked in front of the hotel to the valets waiting there to park cars for guests. The girls spilled out of the SUV, their eyes taking in everything. The hotel, about six stories tall, had impressive floor-to-ceiling windows on the first floor. They sparkled and glittered from all the lights inside, illuminating the red carpet leading into the hotel. They were the first to arrive, so the girls would be early for their coat-check duties. Photographers were gathered around the red carpet, waiting. Lili imagined what it would look like when the guests began to arrive, walking down the carpet as the photographers' flashes went off. They were really a part of this magical night!

"Okay, girls," Mrs. Albern said. "The coat check is in the lobby — all the guests will pass in front of it to get to the ballroom." She had gone over their duties with them earlier in the day.

The Jewels hurried inside and set up in the coat-check stand. The wide, double doors had a cutout from which the girls could talk to guests and take their coats. The large closet was filled with bars holding empty hangers. There was room for hundreds of coats. Once inside, Willow took out the box of numbered tags.

"Remember," she told the other girls. "There are two of each number. The guest gets one number to keep, and the other will get hung on the hanger with the coat."

Erin stood by the door, gazing out into the hotel lobby. "We've got a perfect view from here," she said. "We can see the front door, the elevators, the red carpet leading to the ballroom, and the door leading to the hotel's stairs. If the Rivals show up tonight, we'll spot them!"

A steady stream of guests began to arrive a few minutes later, and the girls became busy taking coats. Each gown was more opulent than the last, as all the socialites in town had been invited. The next stop after the coat check was the step and repeat — a place where all the guests were photographed before heading into the ballroom. The girls watched the guests pose amid the flash of camera bulbs.

"Wow! I feel like I'm at the Academy Awards," Lili said dreamily as she watched.

Willow was checking in a coat when she spotted Derrica coming out of the elevator and heading toward the side door. She nudged Lili and pointed at her. "Where's she going?" she asked.

Lili smiled. "She's staying in the hotel, right? I bet she's going to make her grand entrance on the red carpet. She wouldn't miss that!"

Lili was right. After a few moments they heard the reporters calling her name. "Derrica, this way! Derrica, who are you wearing tonight?"

The doorman held open the door and in walked Derrica, radiant in a red, floor-length tiered gown. She wore a ruby and diamond necklace with a diamond ribbon pin fastened at her waist. Since she didn't have a coat, she walked right past the coat check to the step and repeat. A cameraman dressed in a tux filmed her. As she posed, everyone stopped and stared. When she was finished, two women walked over to her. Derrica greeted them both with big air kisses. "Darlings!" she cried. "It's been forever." Then she disappeared with them into the ballroom.

"Derrica really knows how to make an entrance, doesn't she?" Erin remarked. "But what about the Rivals? There's still no sign of them."

Lili held up her phone. "That's going to change. Eli just texted me. Ryan is approaching the hotel!"

The girls all stiffened. Willow's eyes narrowed. "We'll be ready."

They stayed on alert as they continued to check in coats, keeping their eyes glued on the lobby the entire time, wondering how Ryan would try to sneak in.

But Ryan didn't sneak in. Instead, he came strolling in the front door like he owned the hotel, wearing a tux. He was accompanied by a large group of people. The girls recognized his uncle, Arthur Atkinson. The others looked like they must be his parents and other family members. Everyone was dressed up and all the women were dripping with jewels.

"Drat!" Erin fumed. "We should have figured that he would have scored an invite."

Ryan sauntered up to the girls, his black wool coat over his arm. He gave Willow that infuriating, smug smile of his as he gave her his coat. If he was surprised to see them there, he didn't let on.

"Here you go," he said as he handed her a five-dollar bill. Willow felt her blood boil. She handed the money back to him.

"We're volunteering, but thank you anyway," she said stiffly.

He shrugged as he pocketed the money before walking off.

"Ugh!" Erin groaned. "He is king of the creeps!"

Willow nodded. She took a deep breath to calm down. "Yes, but he's probably trying to get under our skin to distract us. Don't let it work."

Erin frowned. "The Rivals always work together. If Ryan is here, I'm sure the others can't be too far away."

"Um, guys?" Lili interrupted. "They're not." She pointed to the door leading to the stairs.

Two figures, dressed all in black, stood in front of the door to the hotel's staircase. They wore black sunglasses and black berets pulled low over their foreheads, clearly as a disguise. The getups may have made them hard to recognize in footage from a security camera, but the Jewels would have recognized them anywhere — it was Aaron and Isabel! Aaron pulled open the door, and they both disappeared into the staircase.

"They are headed upstairs. That's where Derrica's room is! They must be going to steal the emerald," Lili cried. "We've got to stop them!"

Chapter Sixteen

While Willow, Erin, and Lili had been getting ready for the ball, Jasmine had been sitting at home, lost in thought.

"Are you sure you're not going to help out at the charity ball tonight?" Jasmine's mother asked her. Mrs. Albern had called her to let her know the plans.

Jasmine sighed. "I don't think so, Mom," she said.

Mrs. Johnson gave her a hug. "Friends fight sometimes, sweetie. It will be okay, you'll see."

Her mom stood up. "See if you can get around to folding your laundry today, Jasmine, okay?"

"Sure, Mom," Jasmine said gloomily.

It had been a terrible week for Jasmine. She was so angry she didn't want to talk to Willow, even after Willow had apologized to her. But as the days dragged on, she missed her friends. She missed studying for quiz bowl. She missed being in on the plans to stop the Rivals. She missed everything!

With a sigh, she started to fold the pile of clothes on her bed. The first thing she picked up was a red T-shirt. Jasmine turned it inside out and read the words "Jewels Rule!"

Jasmine felt tears start to form. She wanted to wear that shirt again. To be a part of the Jewels. To be with her friends. Right now, they were probably at the hotel, guarding Derrica's room. . . .

Derrica's room. There were a lot of rooms in that hotel, Jasmine knew. Which one was Derrica's? Had the Jewels thought to find out? And how would you learn something like that, anyway?

That settled it. She had to help them — or the Rivals would surely get the emerald.

She took a deep breath and walked to her bedroom door.

"Mom, I changed my mind!" she called down.

Back at the hotel, the rest of the Jewels were ready to go after Isabel and Aaron. "We have to beat them to Derrica's room!" Willow said. She slipped out of the coat closet. "Who's coming with me?"

"I'll go," Erin volunteered. "But Lili should stay here. We can't all leave the coat check."

They quickly agreed to the plan and Lili held up her phone. "I'll keep my phone handy. Text me if you need backup."

"Okay, and if you spot Aaron and Isabel before we get back, text us and let us know," Willow said.

Willow and Erin took off running through the lobby when Willow stopped suddenly.

"Wait a second," she said. "We don't know which room is Derrica's!"

Erin groaned as she slapped her hand to her forehead. "We were so worried about everything else that we forgot the most important detail."

"Okay, let's not panic." Willow tried to stay calm. "We made a mistake, but now we've got to figure out which room Derrica is staying in as quickly as possible."

As Willow and Erin were trying to decide what to do next, Lili waited nervously at the coat check. Lili's eyes grew wide as she watched Rhianna of *East Coast Class* walk through the door. A cameraman was following her, too, filming her every move.

As if there wasn't enough drama, here comes more, Lili thought.

Rhianna sashayed over to the coat check and removed her full-length coat. Lili gasped when she saw what Rhianna was wearing — the same strapless, cream-colored gown that Derrica had bought from Elan last week! *There's going to be trouble*, Lili thought.

"Here you go, darling," Rhianna said as she handed her coat to Lili.

"I love your dress," Lili told her. "It's beautiful."

"Thanks," Rhianna said with a smile. "I had it made especially for me."

Lili handed her the coat-check ticket and watched Rhianna head to the step and repeat. She posed like a pro, laughing and joking with the photographers.

At that exact moment, Derrica emerged from the ballroom. A shocked look spread across her face as she noticed Rhianna wearing her supposedly one-of-a-kind dress.

"You!" Derrica gasped as she rushed over to Rhianna. "Where did you get that dress?"

"Oh, this?" Rhianna asked innocently. "It was made for me by a dear friend, Elan. Perhaps you know him?"

Derrica stomped her foot. "Of course I know him. Don't play dumb with me, Rhianna. You know Elan designs all of my gowns. And he designed the one you're wearing for ME!"

Rhianna smiled. "You must be mistaken, my dear."

"Oh, really?" Derrica asked. She pulled out her phone. "I've got a photo of myself in this gown. See?" She pushed her phone in front of Rhianna's face.

Rhianna squinted her eyes as she peered at the phone. "That looks nothing like my dress!" she announced loudly as she began to back away from Derrica.

Derrica's eyes narrowed. "I should have known better than to believe that phony apology you gave me at lunch the other day. You're not happy unless you're making trouble!"

Rhianna looked angry. "Keep it up, Derrica. And I'll make sure you're kept off the guest list at every party in this town."

"Ha!" Derrica shouted. "As if you could. I know for a fact you weren't invited here tonight. How did you get in? Did you use a fake name or something?"

As Rhianna and Derrica battled it out, Jasmine came running into the hotel. She stopped short when she heard the reality stars' shouts echoing throughout the lobby. She noticed the two young women working the front desk were intently watching the fight unfold as they whispered to each other.

"That's Derrica from *East Coast Class*," one said to the other. "I wish I could hear what they were saying!"

Jasmine had an idea. She walked up to the clerks.

"If you want, I'll keep an eye on the desk for you while you get closer to the action," Jasmine suggested. "If anyone comes, I'll run and get you right away."

The women exchanged glances. "We really shouldn't, but I don't want to miss this," one woman said. "Thanks!" They both hurried off to get a closer look as Jasmine moved behind the desk and began typing on the hotel computer.

Meanwhile, Erin and Willow were still trying to figure out how to get Derrica's room number.

"We can ask at the front desk," Erin suggested. "But they wouldn't give out that kind of info to us."

"We've got to try!" Willow said. "Let's hurry."

They raced over to the front desk. "Excuse me," Erin panted. "We need your help. It's really important!"

Jasmine peered out from behind the computer. "I always help my friends," she said with a smile.

"Jasmine?" Willow asked, shocked. "Look, I'm really sorry —"

"No time!" Jasmine said. "We'll talk later. Right now you need the room number, right?"

Erin and Willow nodded.

"It's room six twenty-five. Now hurry!" Jasmine said.

Willow raced toward the staircase, Erin right behind her. "Wait!" Erin yelled. "The elevator will probably be faster."

Willow was a quick runner, but six flights was a lot. Together they ran over to the elevator and Willow hit the up button. The doors opened and they hurried inside. The elevator ride seemed to take forever. Willow tapped her foot impatiently the entire time but finally the doors slid open on the sixth floor. They rushed into the hallway and followed the signs to room 625.

"Of course it had to be the room farthest away," Erin complained as they ran past room 600 first. The hotel room numbers flew by them as they pounded down the hall until they reached the end, where they had to turn right for room 625. They rounded the corner just in time to see Isabel and Aaron coming out of Derrica's suite. They skidded to a halt and stopped right in front of them.

"Nice outfits," Erin said bitingly. "Where did you get them, the costume store?"

Aaron laughed. He was gripping something in his hand tightly. Willow saw a gold chain peeking out from between his fingers. It was the necklace!

They stood for a minute, staring at each other.

No one was sure what to do next, until Isabel broke the tension.

"You'll never win!" she cried. Then she and Aaron took off running.

Willow and Erin raced after them. The chase was on!

Chapter Seventeen

Back at the coat check, Lili anxiously scanned the hallway for any sign of Willow and Erin.

What if the Rivals get the necklace? she thought. *The Rivals already have the ruby and the diamond, and maybe even the sapphire. If they get the emerald tonight, it's all over.*

Lili took a deep breath and decided to distract herself with glamour. She peered into the ballroom. It was filled with party guests in stunning dresses and crisp tuxedoes. Ninjalike servers slipped between the crowd, carrying silver trays of food that looked like tiny pieces of art. In the background, a jazz band played smooth music.

Willow's mom is so lucky to be there, Lili mused dreamily. *And I think she looks perfect. Some of these people are just too overdressed.*

"Earth to Lili!" Jasmine said, waving her palm in front of Lili's face.

Lili jumped. "Jasmine!" she cried as she ran over to give her friend a big hug.

"I thought you guys might need my help, so I came by," Jasmine said. She filled Lili in on the room number, then Lili told her about Isabel and Aaron.

"I'm sure they've got it under control," Lili said. "But thank heavens you showed up!"

Then a tone rang from Lili's cell phone.

"Oh, wait," Lili said, flipping it open. "Willow's texting me now."

Willow and Erin followed Aaron and Isabel as they raced through the twisting hallways, turning right, then left, then right again. Willow, the fastest runner, had quickly sprinted ahead of Erin and then Isabel. Aaron was just a few feet away.

"Tackle him before he gets to the stairs!" Erin yelled.

Heart pounding, Willow pushed forward like she was in a race and Aaron was at the finish line. She reached out to grab him when suddenly she felt her legs give way beneath her.

Slam! She fell facedown onto the carpeted floor. Then she heard a laugh and the *thud* of a heavy door closing.

Erin ran up and knelt down beside her.

"What happened?" Willow asked, dazed.

"Isabel tripped you," Erin said grimly. "You okay?"

"Sure," Willow said, but she winced as she got to her feet. "Scratch that. My ankle's twisted. Erin, get them!"

"Me?" Erin asked. Willow was always the one who did the super-hero athletic stuff.

"I'll text Lili and tell her to watch the front," Willow said. "Now, go!"

Erin turned and raced to the staircase. The sound of Aaron and Isabel's footsteps echoed from a few floors below. Looking down, Erin could see the top of Isabel's blond head. Then she heard the sound of a door opening.

By the time Erin reached the door, Aaron and Isabel had gone through it. She pushed it open and looked in both directions. Had she lost them?

Then she noticed that a swinging door down on the right was still moving back and forth.

They must have gone through there, Erin realized. She sped to the door and pushed inside.

The sound of steam hissing, clanging pots and pans, and shouting voices assaulted her and she entered the busy hotel kitchen. Men and women in white chef's jackets and hats busily worked at stations along rows of gleaming stainless-steel tables and ovens. They were so busy that they didn't notice Aaron quietly weaving his way between them, heading for the next exit.

"Stop that boy! He's a thief!" Erin yelled, but her voice couldn't be heard over the din. She sprinted across the floor, darting from left to right around the chefs like a soccer player dribbling down a field.

Wait a second. Where's Isabel? she thought.

Splat! Something cold and mushy hit her in the face, and Erin stopped, stunned. When she got her bearings she wiped some of the mess off and got a good look at it.

"Cake?" she asked, wiping the frosting from her eyes.

That's when she saw Isabel standing in front of her, grinning.

"Face it, Erin," Isabel said in her French accent. "You will always lose."

As she spoke, a tall, red-faced chef marched up behind her. Erin grinned.

"Maybe not," Erin said. Then she quickly darted to the next row of workstations as the angry chef grabbed Isabel by the arm.

"What are you doing in my kitchen?" he bellowed.

Erin would have loved to stay to see the look on Isabel's face, but she knew she had to get to Aaron.

"Excuse me. Pardon me. Excuse me," she said politely, making her way through the chefs. They didn't even bat an eye at the girl with cake on her face.

Erin finally pushed through the kitchen doors just in time to see Aaron making a right turn down the hallway. She ran as fast as she could, adrenaline fueling her speed.

Now Aaron was making his way past the coat check, and to Erin's relief she saw Jasmine and Lili standing at the end of the hallway, blocking his way to the door. Then the elevator dinged and opened, and Willow limped out.

Aaron stopped in the middle of the hallway, weighing his options. He looked scared and confused.

"Woo-hoo! We got him!" Erin cheered.

"You have nothing," a deep voice boomed.

Arthur Atkinson stepped out of the ballroom, followed by Ryan. He calmly approached Aaron and put a hand on his shoulder.

"Aaron, Ryan, and I are going to walk out of here, and there is nothing you can do about it," he said smoothly.

"We can yell! We can call the police!" Willow said, her dark eyes flashing angrily.

"Go ahead. See who believes you," Arthur said. Then he swiftly ushered Aaron and Ryan out the door and into a waiting limousine.

Erin raced up to meet her friends.

"It's not fair!" she wailed. "We should have . . . we could have . . ."

"Arthur's right," Jasmine said sadly. "We've accused the Rivals of stealing a jewel before, and we only got humiliated for it."

Willow limped back into the coat check and sunk to the ground, defeated. She put her head in her hands.

Erin curled her hand into a fist and shook it into the air.

"You wanna know how the Atkinson family got so rich?" she asked angrily. "They probably made their fortune by other people paying them to stay away. They are the most infuriating, obnoxious family on the planet!"

Lili shuddered. "What if the Rivals have the sapphire, too?"

The girls all took a moment to think about that.

"Then it's all over," Willow said, her voice muffled from her hands still covering her face.

"We did our best." Lili tried to cheer the group up. "And we came really close to stopping them, too." But even the normally optimistic Lili looked glum.

"But we didn't," Willow said as she pulled her hands away from her face. "The Rivals are playing a serious game. And now more than ever, I think it's a game we just can't win."

Chapter Eighteen

Two days later, the girls sat in the school's cafeteria together. They were still feeling terrible.

Erin picked at the food on her tray.

"Hey, it's meatballs, one of your favorites," Lili pointed out.

"I have no appetite," Erin said as she pushed a meatball aimlessly around her plate.

"I have some cool news." Lili tried to change the subject. "Willow's mom made best-dressed in the paper for the outfit I styled for her!"

"She was totally floored," Willow said. "She is going to recommend you to all of her friends, Lili."

"And that's not the only good thing. I see another silver lining," Lili said with a smile. "And she's sitting right there." She pointed to Jasmine.

Willow smiled in agreement. "Last week when we weren't talking was the worst, Jasmine. Way worse than what happened Saturday night. We've been best friends since kindergarten. I can't imagine not having you around."

"I'm sorry I was so stubborn," Jasmine replied. "I should have talked to you before the charity ball, but it was too hard for me."

"I'm sorry, too. I shouldn't have been so bossy. I totally trust you," Willow explained. "But when I get nervous, I feel like I have to do everything myself or things will go wrong. I promise from now on I'll try to work on that."

"Thanks, Willow." Jasmine grinned. "I appreciate that. We were all under so much pressure, it's no wonder we had a meltdown. And I promise the next time I start to feel upset, I'll talk to you about it instead of blowing up."

Lili beamed. "I'm so happy we're a team again. Win or lose, we stick together!"

The girls huddled together and put their hands in the center for a cheer.

"Goooo, Jewels!"

Ms. Ortiz walked up to their table.

"Hello, girls!" she said. "Principal Frederickson would like to see you in her office."

The girls looked at each other. Had the principal already found out about the emerald?

They got an even bigger surprise when they walked into her office — and saw Derrica Girard sitting there!

"Please sit down, girls," Principal Frederickson said.

The four Jewels obeyed, stunned.

"Don't look so scared, girls," Derrica said with a smile. "You're not in trouble or anything."

Jasmine let out a huge sigh of relief and sank back into her chair.

"That's good," she said.

"But what are you doing here?" Willow asked. "We never told you we went to this school."

"It's all very interesting," Principal Frederickson explained. "You see, I had been trying to reach Derrica to talk to her about the emerald."

"And then yesterday, when I realized it was stolen, my publicist finally told me that your principal had called," Derrica went on. "She hadn't taken it seriously until that point. Then when Alicia and I talked, and she told me she was a school principal, I remembered that two schoolgirls had tried to warn me about the emerald being stolen. I mentioned it to her and, well, here we are."

"Alicia?" Lili muttered with a curious look. It was difficult to imagine the stern principal having a first name, for some reason.

Willow looked at Principal Frederickson. "Does she know about the Martha Washington jewels?"

The principal nodded. "I told her. I think she deserves to know."

"It's really amazing," Derrica said, with a wave of her blond hair. "That emerald has been in my family for years. I always knew it was special, but I never knew that it was an important part of history."

"But now Arthur Atkinson has it," Erin pointed out. "So you can tell the police and get it back from him, right?"

"Wait a moment," Principal Frederickson interrupted. "How do you know for sure that Arthur is responsible for stealing the emerald on Saturday?"

The girls looked at each other. There was no point in keeping the secret now.

"We were working coat check at the ball that night," Erin said. "We saw Aaron and Isabel head up to Derrica's room. Aaron got the necklace. We almost stopped him, but then Arthur Atkinson stepped in and they all escaped."

Principal Frederickson looked like she was about to scold them, but Derrica spoke up first.

"I know Arthur," she said with a frown. "We used to travel in the same circles. He is a conniving, ruthless man. I'm not sure if going to the police would do any good. After all, you girls are the only witnesses, and . . ."

Erin sighed. "I know. We're just a bunch of kids. Nobody takes us seriously."

"So you're just going to let him have it?" Jasmine asked in disbelief.

Now it was Derrica's turn to sigh. "I don't know. Maybe he'll give it back after he's done doing . . . whatever it is he's doing with those stones."

"The Martha Washington diary says that the four stones hold a secret," Erin said. "We know he has the ruby, the diamond, and now the emerald. If he has the sapphire, too, there is no use trying to stop him now. He'll have everything he needs."

The four girls looked miserable as Erin's words sank in. It was all over!

But Derrica shook her head. "That's the thing. I don't think he does have the sapphire," she said.

Willow's eyes widened. "But how do you know for sure?"

"Well, Elan was telling me that Arthur's going around to all of the jewelers and clothiers asking about a certain type of sapphire," Derrica explained. "I remember he was always angry about the Atkinson sapphire being stolen all those years ago. I assumed that he's still looking for it, but now that I know about the Martha Washington jewels, his search suddenly means something very different."

"He probably is," Willow said, looking excited again for the first time since the emerald was stolen. "And if he doesn't have the sapphire yet, then he doesn't have the four clues that he needs."

Jasmine almost jumped out of her chair. "Derrica, I just thought of something. The diamond had a clue etched on the back of it. Did you ever see anything on the back of the emerald?"

"No," Derrica said. "It was always in its setting. I never looked at the back of it."

Everyone was silent for a moment.

"Of course," Principal Frederickson said slowly, "you girls will stay out of this in the future, as you've promised, correct?"

"Gee, they seem like pretty good detectives to me," Derrica said, grinning at the girls. "Did you really chase those necklace thieves through the hotel?"

"Erin and Willow did most of the chasing," Lili said. "Erin got a faceful of cake, and Willow twisted her ankle."

"It's pretty much better, really," Willow said in response to Principal Frederickson's horrified look.

"This is exactly why I wanted you girls to stay out of this," the principal said fretfully.

"We can't stop now," Erin pleaded. "We've come this far."

"Well, I, for one, am going to start looking for that sapphire," Derrica said. "If Arthur Atkinson thinks he can steal my emerald from me, he's got another thing coming. I will beat him at his own game. If I find the sapphire, maybe we can trade it for the emerald. I'm not losing my lucky necklace to that man. And I wouldn't mind getting some help from some whip-smart sixth-grade girls. You have proven yourselves to be super detectives. I'm impressed!"

Erin quickly took out her phone. "I'll send you my number through your Chatter page. If we find out anything, we'll let you know."

"And I'll do the same," Derrica promised.

Principal Frederickson was clearly rattled. "I need to think about this. Girls, please head to your classes."

"It was really nice to meet you," Jasmine said shyly to Derrica.

"And if you want any ideas for what to wear to that movie premiere, let me know," Lili added. "I just got one of my clients onto the best-dressed list."

Derrica raised an eyebrow. "My, you girls have many talents, don't you?"

"That other dress wasn't your color, anyway," Lili went on. "And I think a slimmer cut would be —"

But Principal Frederickson's glare made her stop. The girls quickly left the office, calling good-bye behind them.

When they got back into the hall they walked a little way and then stopped in the alcove by the water fountain.

"This is amazing!" Erin said. "Derrica is, like, our friend!"

"It's too bad we couldn't save the emerald for her," Jasmine remarked. "You know, I was thinking. Last time when we got the diamond, we had help from whoever it was who left us those notes on yellow paper. I wonder why we didn't get any this time?"

"Yeah, that is weird," Lili said. "We sure could have used it."

"We don't need help," Willow said, her voice filled with confidence. "We have each other. And Eli. We're smart. Smart enough to get the sapphire before the Rivals do. This time, we're going to win!"

"And we'll do it *together*," Erin said, eyeing Jasmine. "Right?"

Jasmine grinned. "Right!"

Help the
JEWELS
with their next heist!

JEWEL thieves

battle of the brightest

Hope McLean

■SCHOLASTIC

Turn the page for a super secret sneak peek at the fourth book in the Jewel Thieves series!

The Andover Mansion was impressive, and Willow quickly counted over thirty windows in the front of the house. It had a huge lawn and a circular driveway, complete with a fountain in the middle.

Erin read from her phone. "Derrica said to go to the French doors off the library at four p.m. Then we're supposed to walk around to the back of the house, and the library will be located to our left."

Guests were already driving up and valets were parking their cars for them. The team decided to walk on the far side of the lawn, which had a row of trees planted next to the driveway, so as not to draw any attention to themselves.

They rounded the house and came to the backyard, where they saw the gleaming glass French doors, just as Derrica had described. Eli reached his hand to the doorknob and turned it, but the door was locked.

"Did Derrica forget?" Erin asked, panicked.

If Derrica didn't come through, they would miss their chance to talk to Mr. Andover!

The handle of the door slowly turned. Derrica poked her head out. "Just in time!" she said in a loud whisper. "Mr. Andover is in the library."

They all exchanged excited glances. Answers to all their questions about the sapphire could be waiting for them just on the other side of that door!